STONE ARCH BOOKS
a capstone imprint

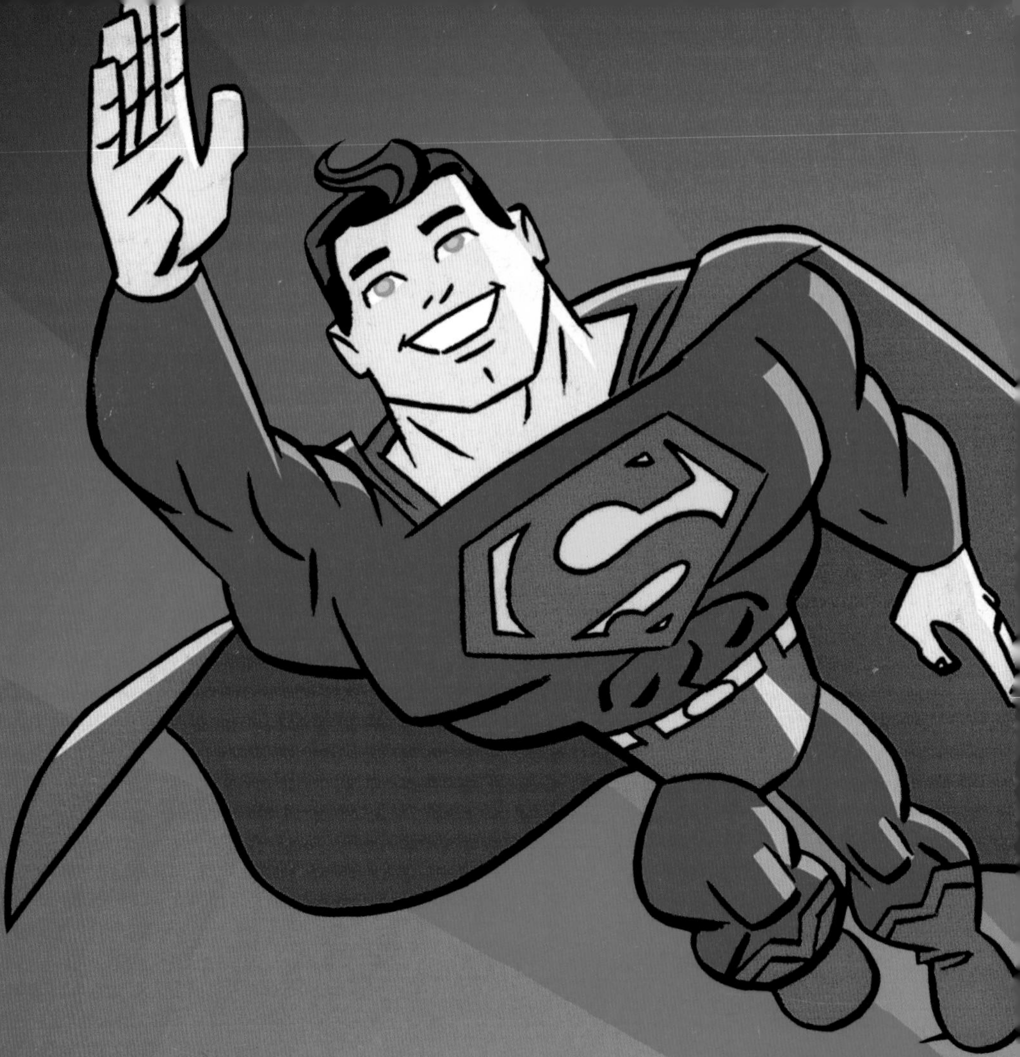

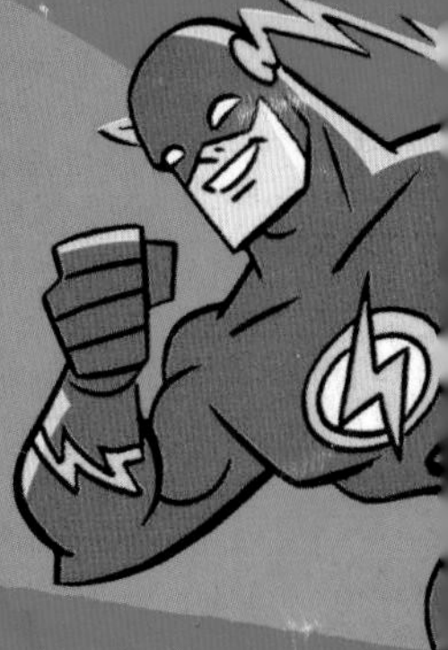

STONE ARCH BOOKS™
Published in 2014
A Capstone Imprint
1710 Roe Crest Drive
North Mankato, MN 56003
www.capstonepub.com

Originally published by DC Comics in the U.S. in single magazine form as DC Super Friends #11.

DC Comics
1700 Broadway, New York, NY 10019
A Warner Bros. Entertainment Company

Cataloging-in-Publication Data is available at the Library of Congress website:
ISBN: 978-1-4342-9224-7 (library binding)

Summary: Batman's got a fan club! Unfortunately, it's run by the mischievous imp known as Bat-Mite, and he just can't stand the fact that he's not alongside Batman "helping" the hero with his magical talents!

STONE ARCH BOOKS
Ashley C. Andersen Zantop *Publisher*
Michael Dahl *Editorial Director*
Sean Tulien *Editor*
Heather Kindseth *Creative Director*
Brann Garvey and Alison Thiele *Designers*
Kathy McColley *Production Specialist*

DC COMICS
Rachel Gluckstern Original U.S. Editor

Printed in China.
032014 008085LEOF14

DC ☆ SUPER FRIENDS

Who is the Mystery Bat-Squad?

Sholly Fisch ....writer
Chynna Clugston ....illustrator
Heroic Age ....colorist
J. Bone ....cover artist
Travis Lanham.....................letterer

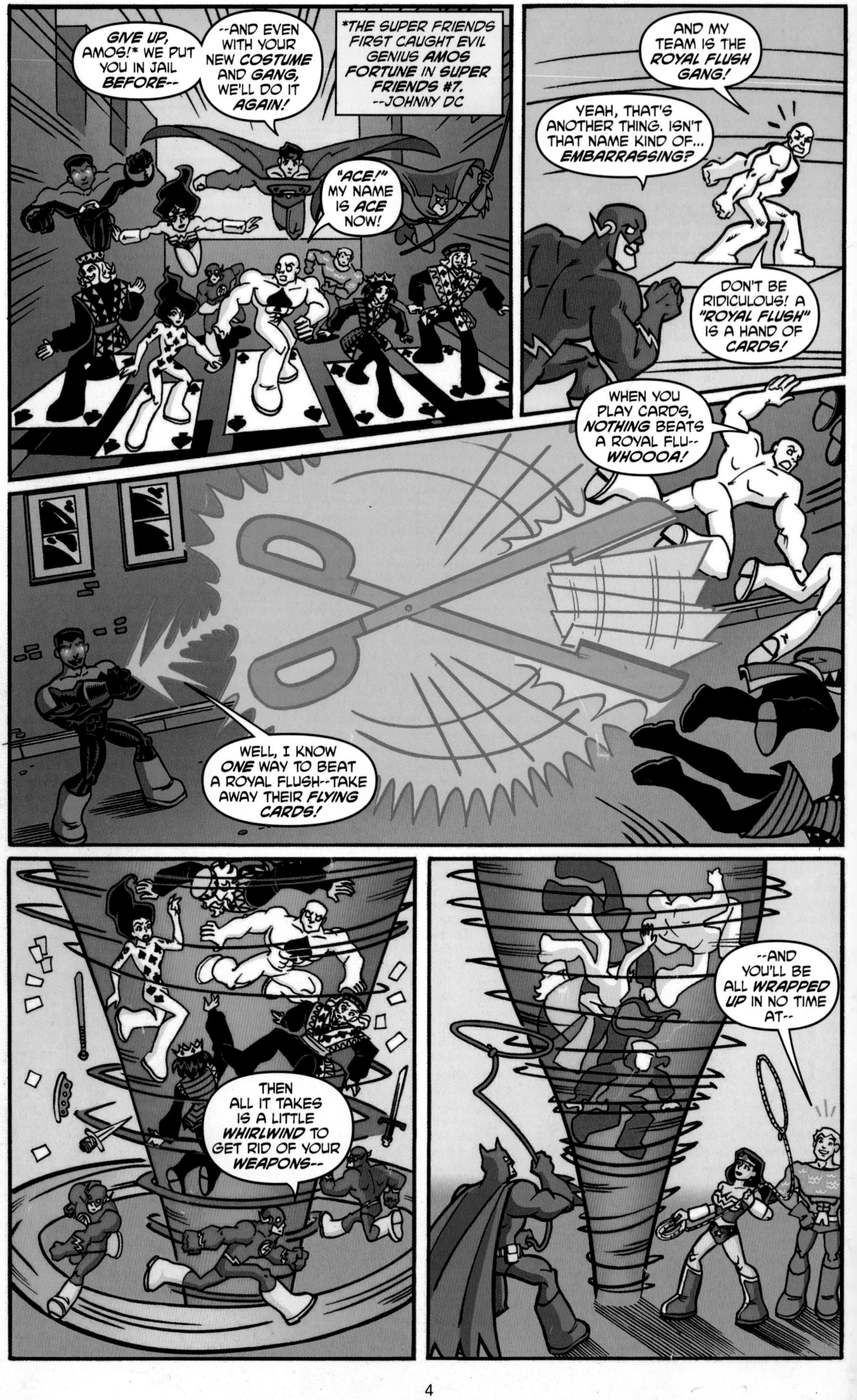
GIVE UP, AMOS!* WE PUT YOU IN JAIL BEFORE--
--AND EVEN WITH YOUR NEW COSTUME AND GANG, WE'LL DO IT AGAIN!
*THE SUPER FRIENDS FIRST CAUGHT EVIL GENIUS AMOS FORTUNE IN SUPER FRIENDS #7. --JOHNNY DC
"ACE!" MY NAME IS ACE NOW!
AND MY TEAM IS THE ROYAL FLUSH GANG!
YEAH, THAT'S ANOTHER THING. ISN'T THAT NAME KIND OF... EMBARRASSING?
DON'T BE RIDICULOUS! A "ROYAL FLUSH" IS A HAND OF CARDS!
WHEN YOU PLAY CARDS, NOTHING BEATS A ROYAL FLU-- WHOOOA!
WELL, I KNOW ONE WAY TO BEAT A ROYAL FLUSH--TAKE AWAY THEIR FLYING CARDS!
THEN ALL IT TAKES IS A LITTLE WHIRLWIND TO GET RID OF YOUR WEAPONS--
--AND YOU'LL BE ALL WRAPPED UP IN NO TIME AT--

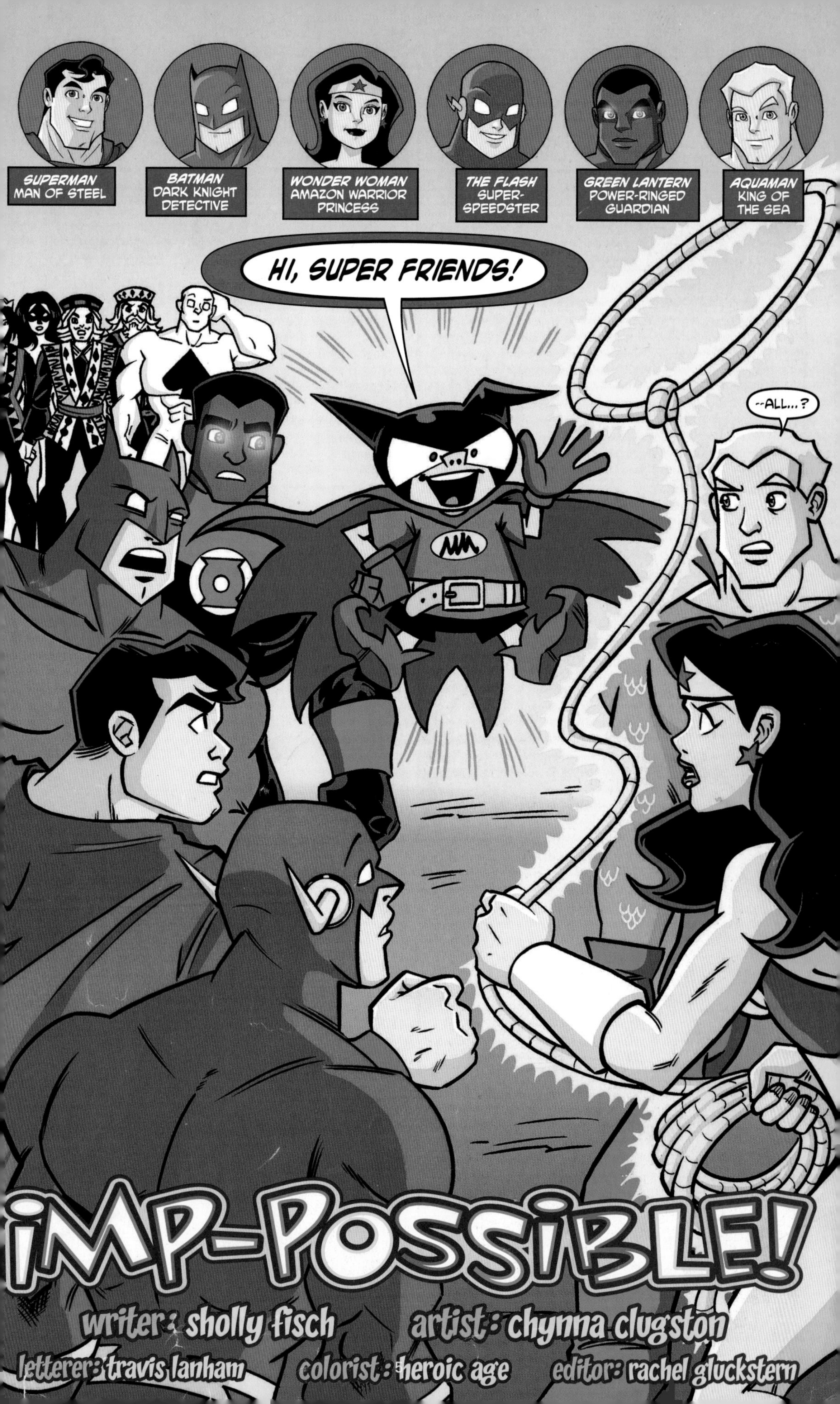
SUPERMAN
MAN OF STEEL
BATMAN
DARK KNIGHT DETECTIVE
WONDER WOMAN
AMAZON WARRIOR PRINCESS
THE FLASH
SUPER-SPEEDSTER
GREEN LANTERN
POWER-RINGED GUARDIAN
AQUAMAN
KING OF THE SEA
HI, SUPER FRIENDS!
--ALL...?
iMP-POSSiBLE!
writer: sholly fisch
artist: chynna clugston
letterer: travis lanham
colorist: heroic age
editor: rachel gluckstern

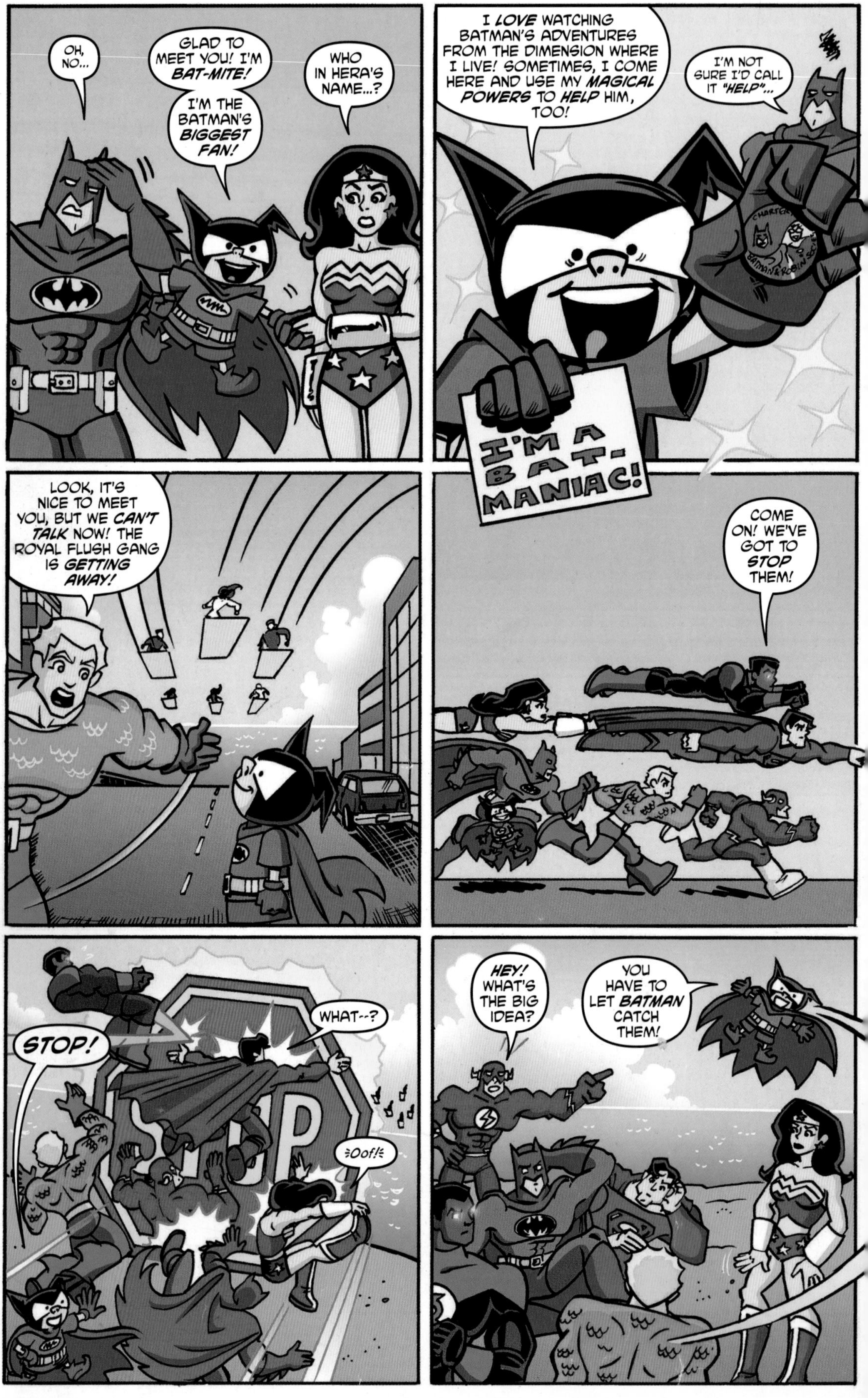
OH, NO...
GLAD TO MEET YOU! I'M BAT-MITE!
I'M THE BATMAN'S BIGGEST FAN!
WHO IN HERA'S NAME...?
I LOVE WATCHING BATMAN'S ADVENTURES FROM THE DIMENSION WHERE I LIVE! SOMETIMES, I COME HERE AND USE MY MAGICAL POWERS TO HELP HIM, TOO!
I'M NOT SURE I'D CALL IT "HELP"...
I'M A BAT-MANIAC!
LOOK, IT'S NICE TO MEET YOU, BUT WE CAN'T TALK NOW! THE ROYAL FLUSH GANG IS GETTING AWAY!
COME ON! WE'VE GOT TO STOP THEM!
STOP!
WHAT--?
Oof!
HEY! WHAT'S THE BIG IDEA?
YOU HAVE TO LET BATMAN CATCH THEM!

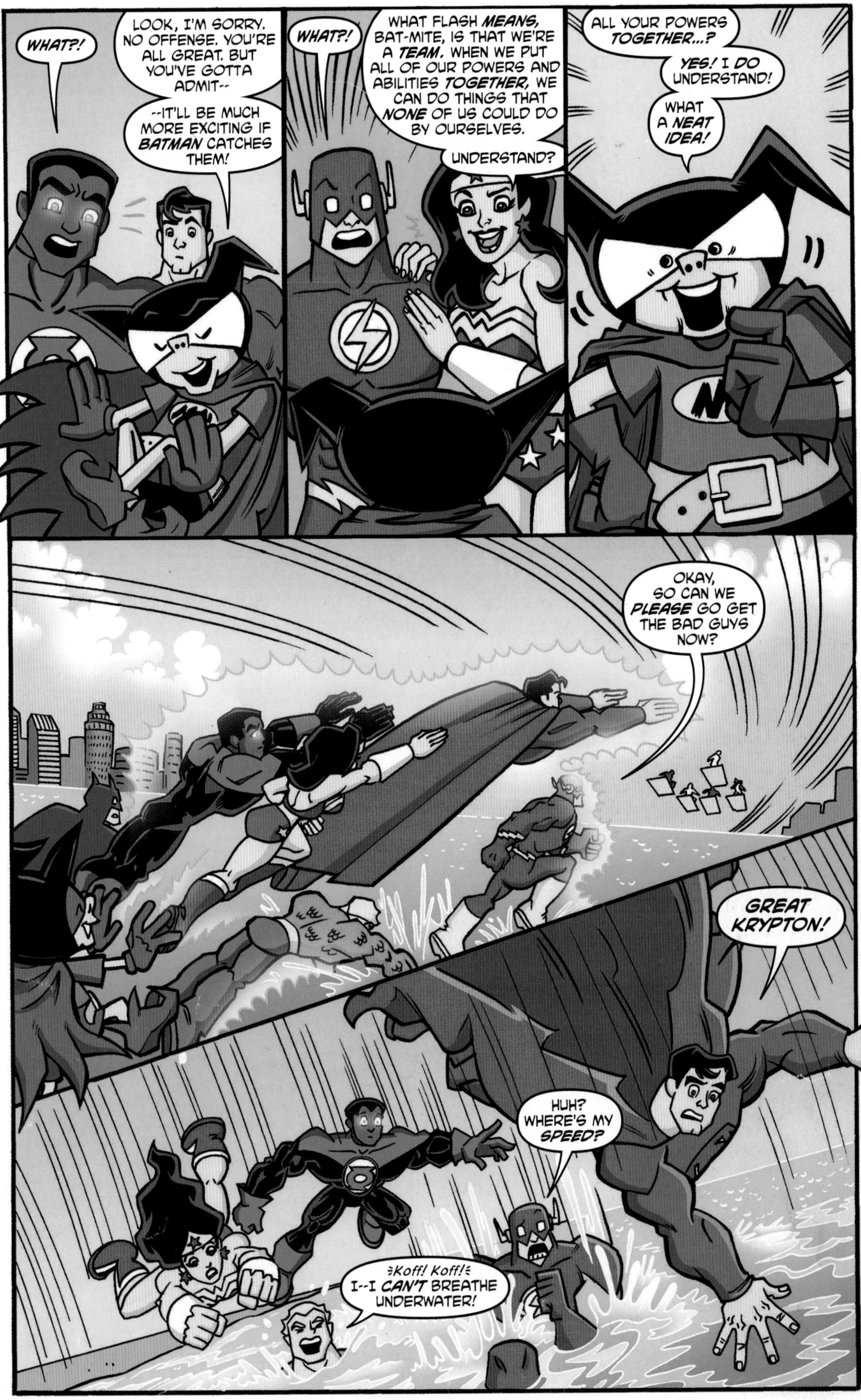
WHAT?!
LOOK, I'M SORRY. NO OFFENSE. YOU'RE ALL GREAT. BUT YOU'VE GOTTA ADMIT--
--IT'LL BE MUCH MORE EXCITING IF BATMAN CATCHES THEM!
WHAT?!
WHAT FLASH MEANS, BAT-MITE, IS THAT WE'RE A TEAM. WHEN WE PUT ALL OF OUR POWERS AND ABILITIES TOGETHER, WE CAN DO THINGS THAT NONE OF US COULD DO BY OURSELVES.
UNDERSTAND?
ALL YOUR POWERS TOGETHER...?
YES! I DO UNDERSTAND!
WHAT A NEAT IDEA!
OKAY, SO CAN WE PLEASE GO GET THE BAD GUYS NOW?
GREAT KRYPTON!
HUH? WHERE'S MY SPEED?
Koff! Koff!
I--I CAN'T BREATHE UNDERWATER!

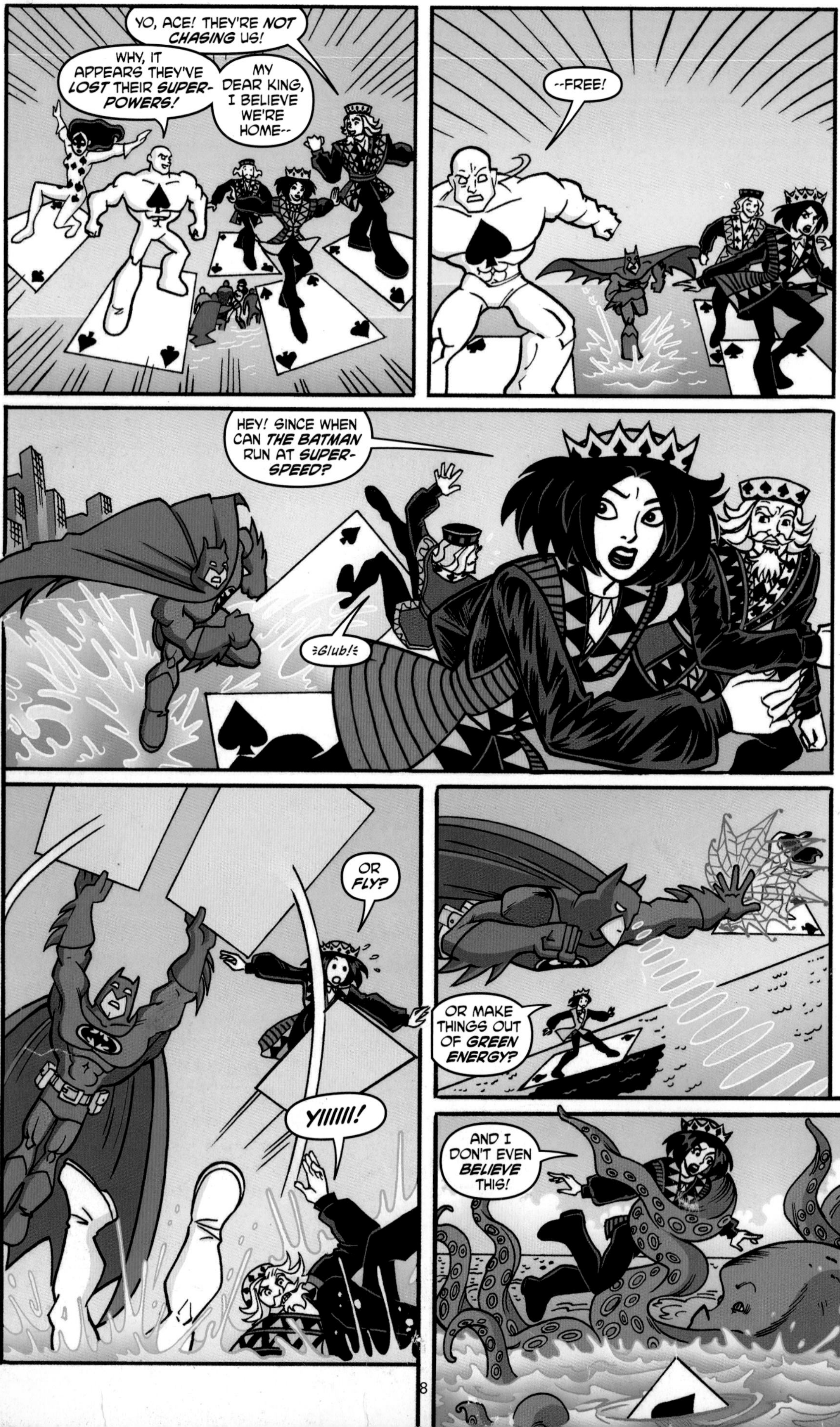
YO, ACE! THEY'RE NOT CHASING US!
WHY, IT APPEARS THEY'VE LOST THEIR SUPER-POWERS!
MY DEAR KING, I BELIEVE WE'RE HOME--
--FREE!
HEY! SINCE WHEN CAN THE BATMAN RUN AT SUPER-SPEED?
Glub!
OR FLY?
YIIIIII!
OR MAKE THINGS OUT OF GREEN ENERGY?
AND I DON'T EVEN BELIEVE THIS!

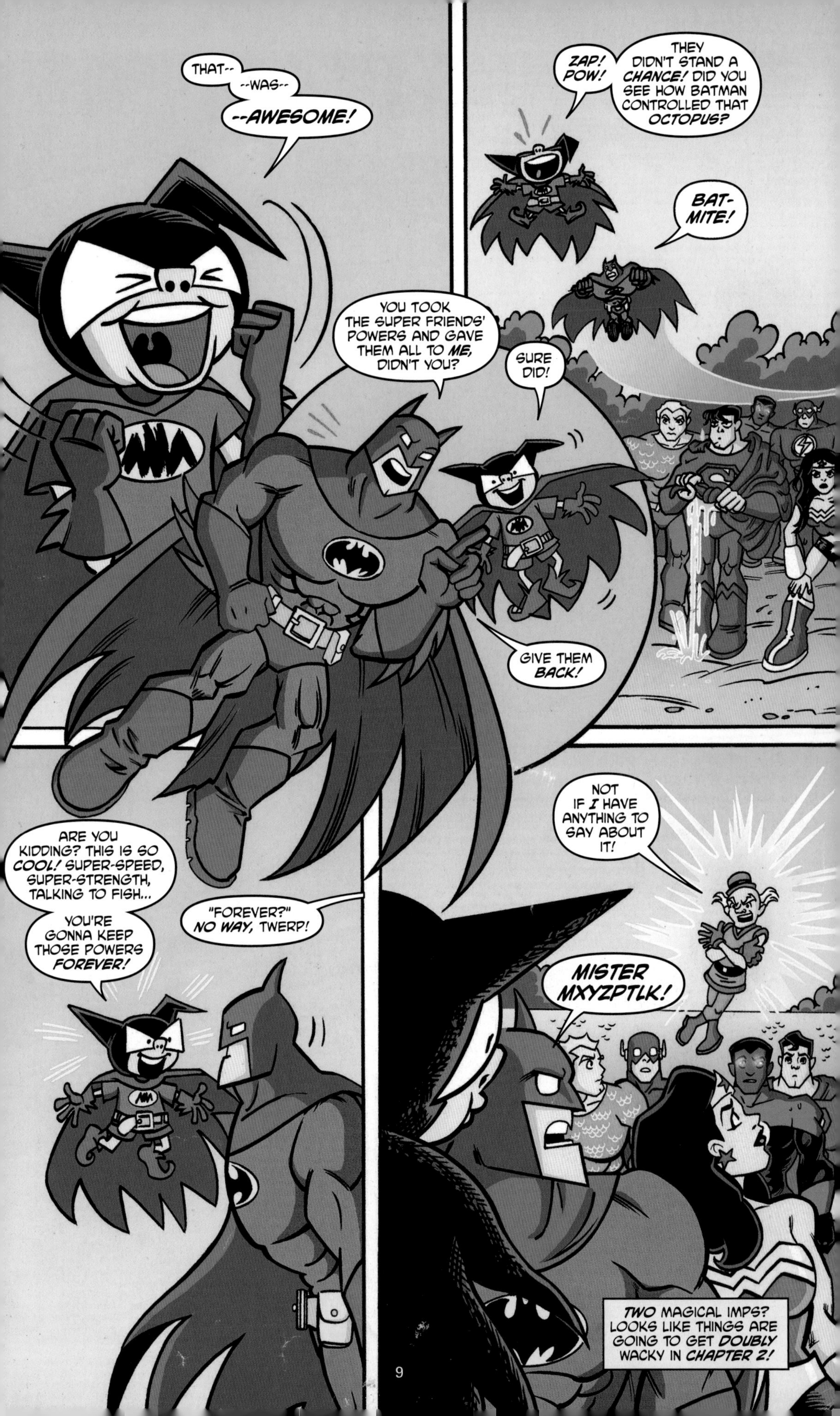
THAT--
--WAS--
--AWESOME!
ZAP! POW!
THEY DIDN'T STAND A CHANCE! DID YOU SEE HOW BATMAN CONTROLLED THAT OCTOPUS?
BAT-MITE!
YOU TOOK THE SUPER FRIENDS' POWERS AND GAVE THEM ALL TO ME, DIDN'T YOU?
SURE DID!
GIVE THEM BACK!
ARE YOU KIDDING? THIS IS SO COOL! SUPER-SPEED, SUPER-STRENGTH, TALKING TO FISH...
YOU'RE GONNA KEEP THOSE POWERS FOREVER!
"FOREVER?" NO WAY, TWERP!
NOT IF I HAVE ANYTHING TO SAY ABOUT IT!
MISTER MXYZPTLK!
TWO MAGICAL IMPS? LOOKS LIKE THINGS ARE GOING TO GET DOUBLY WACKY IN CHAPTER 2!

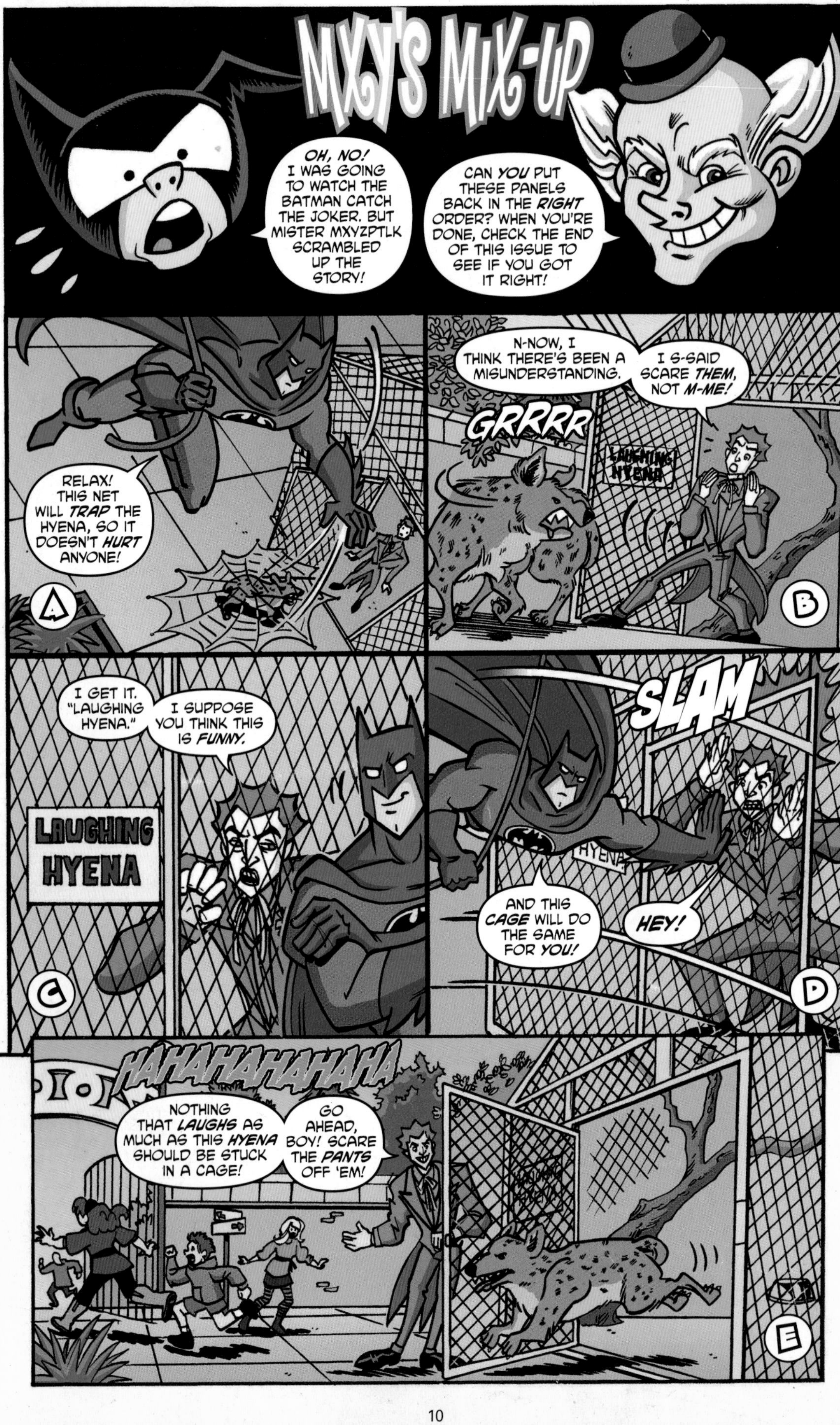
MXY'S MIX-UP
OH, NO! I WAS GOING TO WATCH THE BATMAN CATCH THE JOKER. BUT MISTER MXYZPTLK SCRAMBLED UP THE STORY!
CAN YOU PUT THESE PANELS BACK IN THE RIGHT ORDER? WHEN YOU'RE DONE, CHECK THE END OF THIS ISSUE TO SEE IF YOU GOT IT RIGHT!
RELAX! THIS NET WILL TRAP THE HYENA, SO IT DOESN'T HURT ANYONE!
A
N-NOW, I THINK THERE'S BEEN A MISUNDERSTANDING.
I S-SAID SCARE THEM, NOT M-ME!
GRRRR
LAUGHING HYENA
B
I GET IT. "LAUGHING HYENA."
I SUPPOSE YOU THINK THIS IS FUNNY.
LAUGHING HYENA
C
SLAM
HYENA
AND THIS CAGE WILL DO THE SAME FOR YOU!
HEY!
D
HAHAHAHAHAHAHA
NOTHING THAT LAUGHS AS MUCH AS THIS HYENA SHOULD BE STUCK IN A CAGE!
GO AHEAD, BOY! SCARE THE PANTS OFF 'EM!
E

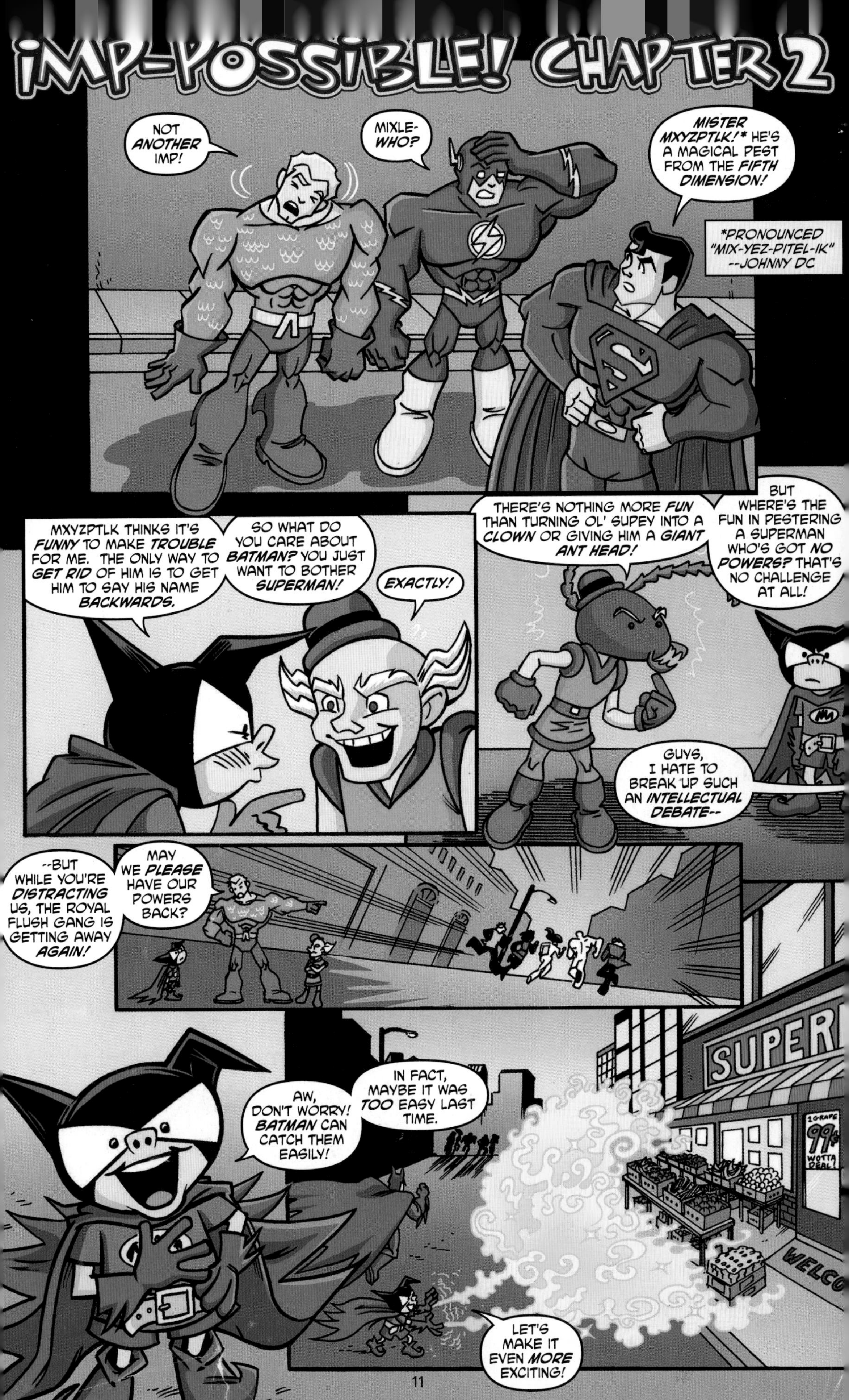
IMP-POSSIBLE! CHAPTER 2
NOT ANOTHER IMP!
MIXLE-WHO?
MISTER MXYZPTLK!* HE'S A MAGICAL PEST FROM THE FIFTH DIMENSION!
*PRONOUNCED "MIX-YEZ-PITEL-IK" --JOHNNY DC
MXYZPTLK THINKS IT'S FUNNY TO MAKE TROUBLE FOR ME. THE ONLY WAY TO GET RID OF HIM IS TO GET HIM TO SAY HIS NAME BACKWARDS.
SO WHAT DO YOU CARE ABOUT BATMAN? YOU JUST WANT TO BOTHER SUPERMAN!
EXACTLY!
THERE'S NOTHING MORE FUN THAN TURNING OL' SUPEY INTO A CLOWN OR GIVING HIM A GIANT ANT HEAD!
BUT WHERE'S THE FUN IN PESTERING A SUPERMAN WHO'S GOT NO POWERS? THAT'S NO CHALLENGE AT ALL!
GUYS, I HATE TO BREAK UP SUCH AN INTELLECTUAL DEBATE--
--BUT WHILE YOU'RE DISTRACTING US, THE ROYAL FLUSH GANG IS GETTING AWAY AGAIN!
MAY WE PLEASE HAVE OUR POWERS BACK?
AW, DON'T WORRY! BATMAN CAN CATCH THEM EASILY!
IN FACT, MAYBE IT WAS TOO EASY LAST TIME.
SUPER
GRAPE 99¢ WOTTA DEAL!
LET'S MAKE IT EVEN MORE EXCITING!

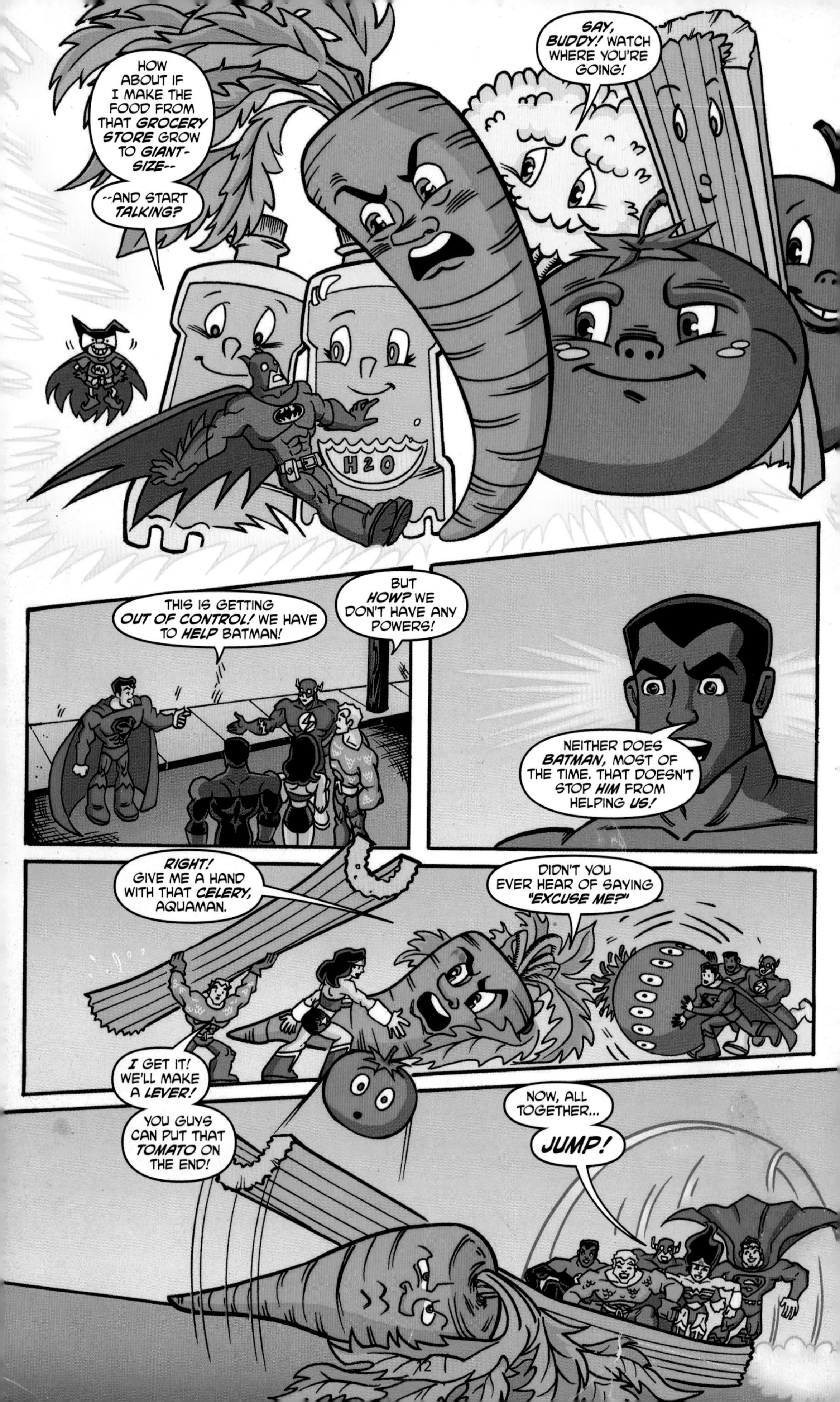
HOW ABOUT IF I MAKE THE FOOD FROM THAT GROCERY STORE GROW TO GIANT-SIZE--
--AND START TALKING?
SAY, BUDDY! WATCH WHERE YOU'RE GOING!
THIS IS GETTING OUT OF CONTROL! WE HAVE TO HELP BATMAN!
BUT HOW? WE DON'T HAVE ANY POWERS!
NEITHER DOES BATMAN, MOST OF THE TIME. THAT DOESN'T STOP HIM FROM HELPING US!
RIGHT! GIVE ME A HAND WITH THAT CELERY, AQUAMAN.
DIDN'T YOU EVER HEAR OF SAYING "EXCUSE ME?"
I GET IT! WE'LL MAKE A LEVER!
YOU GUYS CAN PUT THAT TOMATO ON THE END!
NOW, ALL TOGETHER...
JUMP!
H2O

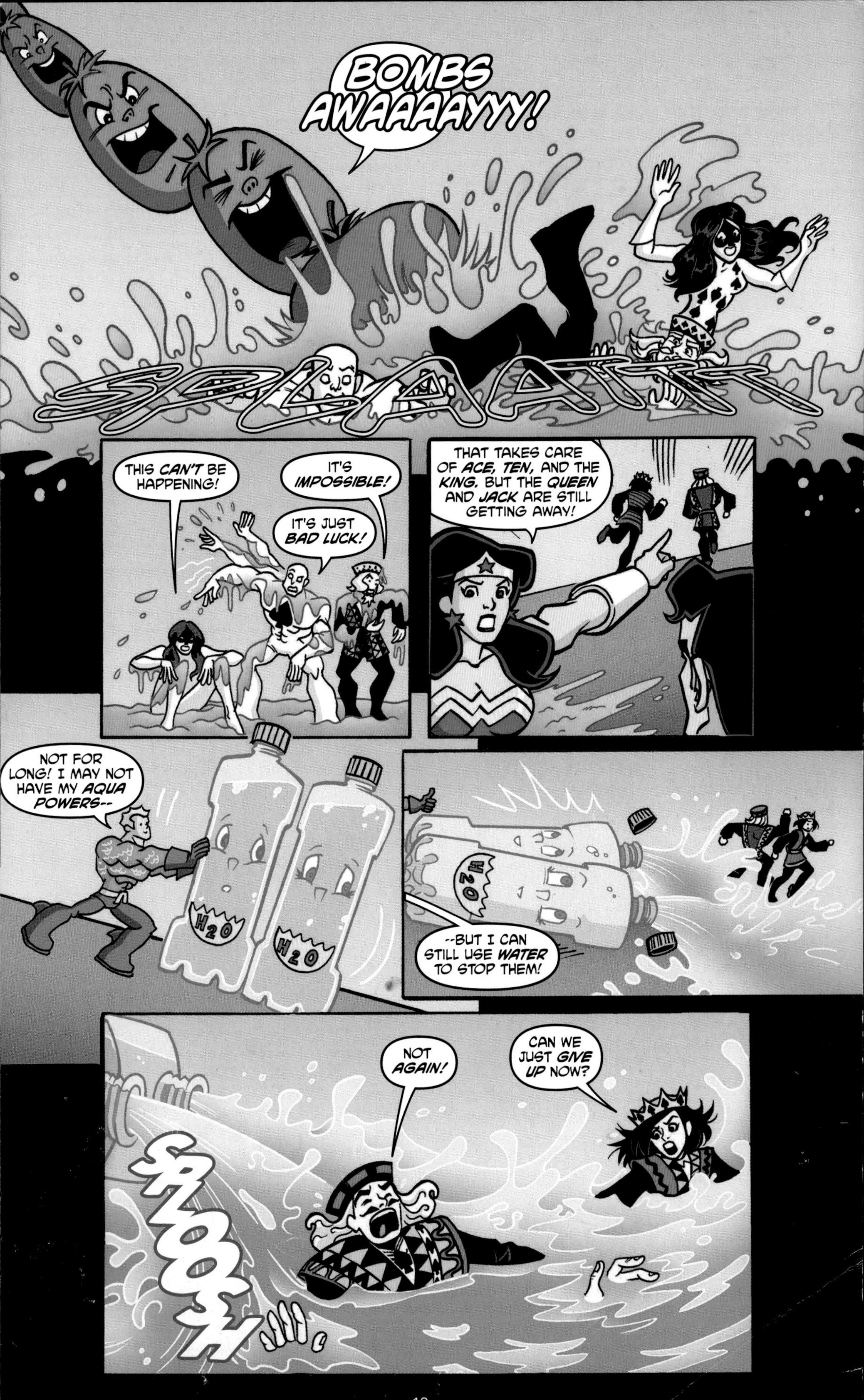
BOMBS AWAAAAAYYY!
SPLAATT
THIS CAN'T BE HAPPENING!
IT'S IMPOSSIBLE!
IT'S JUST BAD LUCK!
THAT TAKES CARE OF ACE, TEN, AND THE KING. BUT THE QUEEN AND JACK ARE STILL GETTING AWAY!
NOT FOR LONG! I MAY NOT HAVE MY AQUA POWERS--
H2O
H2O
--BUT I CAN STILL USE WATER TO STOP THEM!
NOT AGAIN!
CAN WE JUST GIVE UP NOW?
SPLOOSH

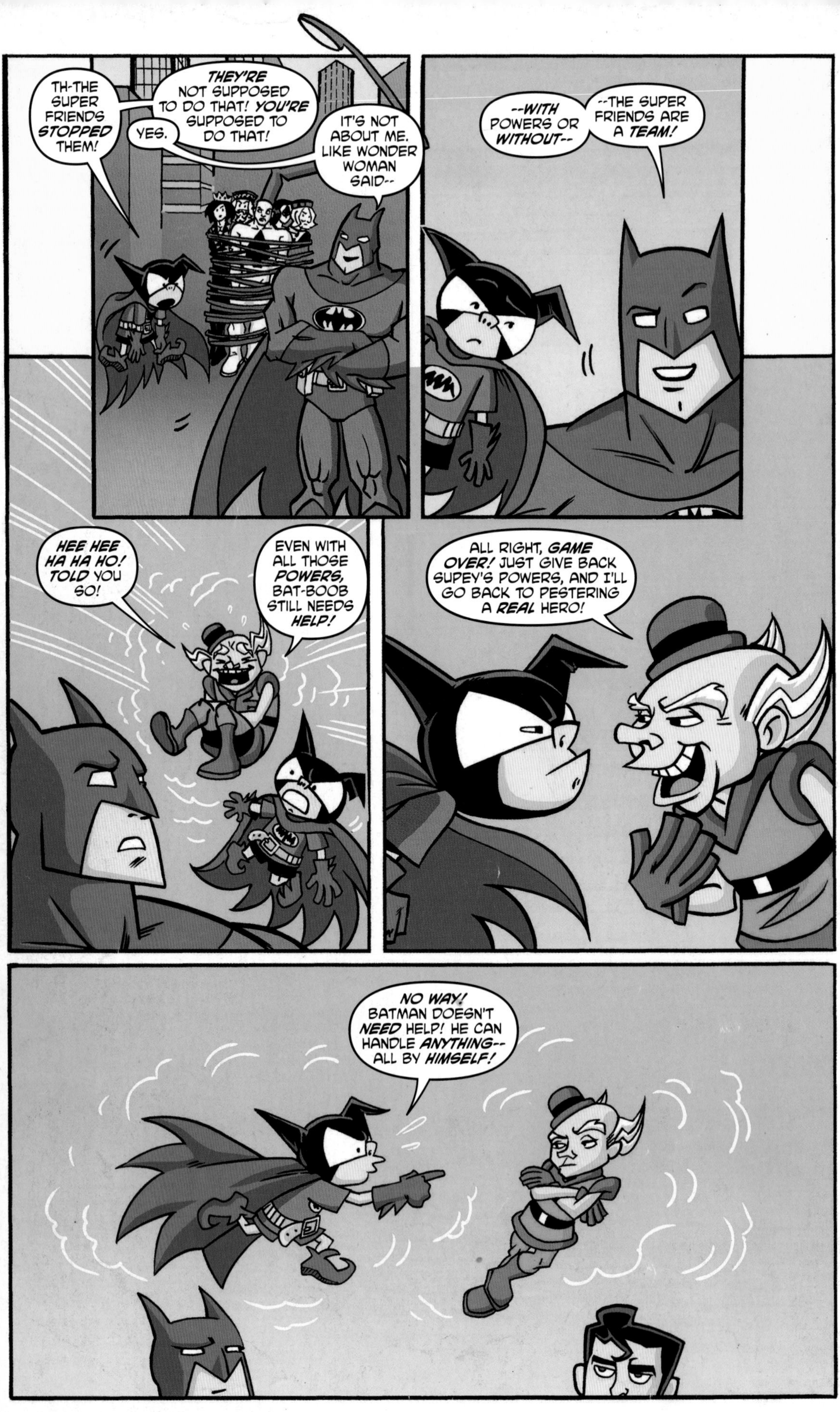

TH-THE SUPER FRIENDS STOPPED THEM!
THEY'RE NOT SUPPOSED TO DO THAT! YOU'RE SUPPOSED TO DO THAT!
YES.
IT'S NOT ABOUT ME. LIKE WONDER WOMAN SAID--
--THE SUPER FRIENDS ARE A TEAM!
--WITH POWERS OR WITHOUT--
HEE HEE HA HA HO! TOLD YOU SO!
EVEN WITH ALL THOSE POWERS, BAT-BOOB STILL NEEDS HELP!
ALL RIGHT, GAME OVER! JUST GIVE BACK SUPEY'S POWERS, AND I'LL GO BACK TO PESTERING A REAL HERO!
NO WAY! BATMAN DOESN'T NEED HELP! HE CAN HANDLE ANYTHING-- ALL BY HIMSELF!

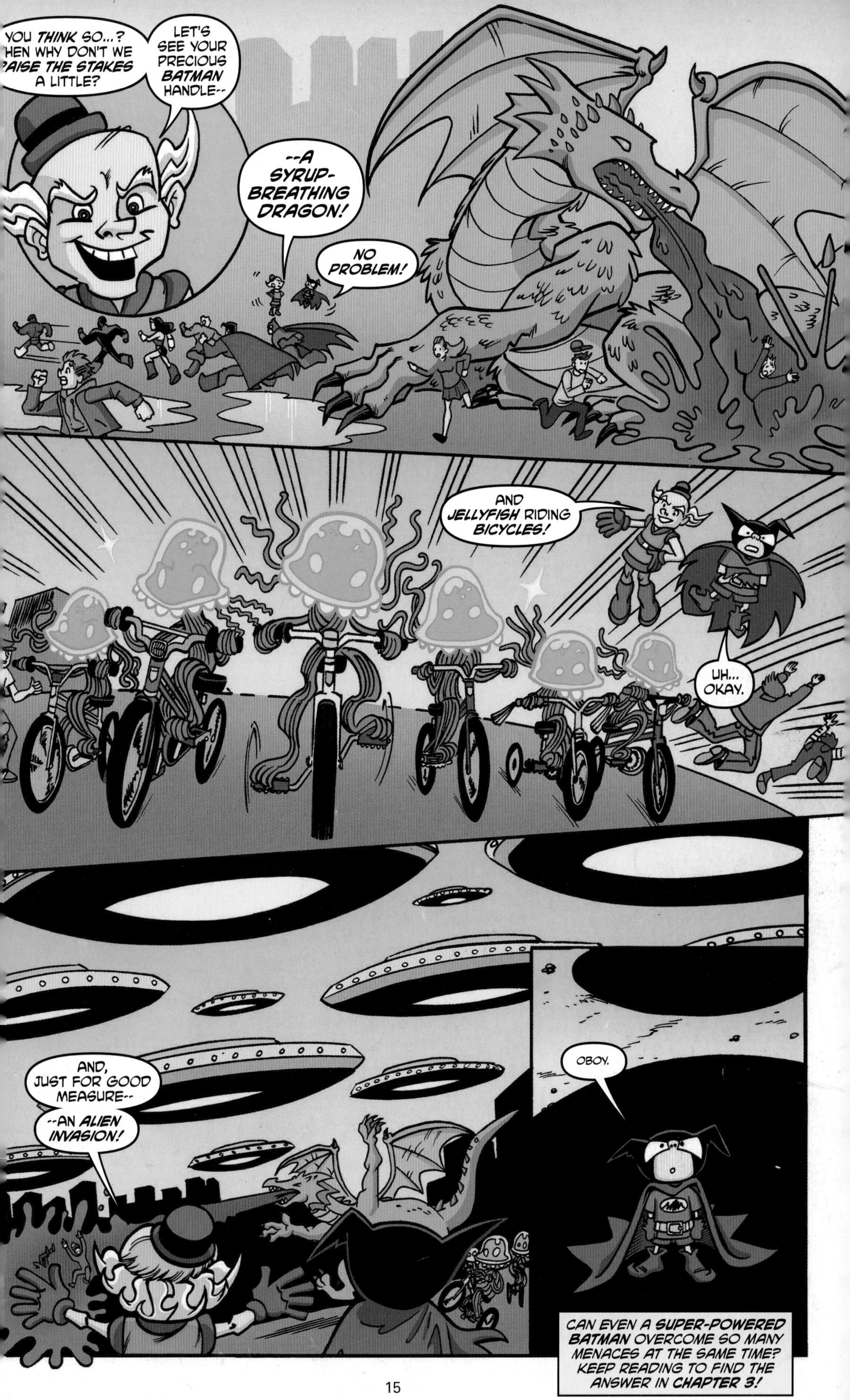
YOU THINK SO...? THEN WHY DON'T WE RAISE THE STAKES A LITTLE?
LET'S SEE YOUR PRECIOUS BATMAN HANDLE--
--A SYRUP-BREATHING DRAGON!
NO PROBLEM!
AND JELLYFISH RIDING BICYCLES!
UH... OKAY.
AND, JUST FOR GOOD MEASURE--
--AN ALIEN INVASION!
OBOY.
CAN EVEN A SUPER-POWERED BATMAN OVERCOME SO MANY MENACES AT THE SAME TIME? KEEP READING TO FIND THE ANSWER IN CHAPTER 3!

IMP-POSSIBLE! CHAPTER 3

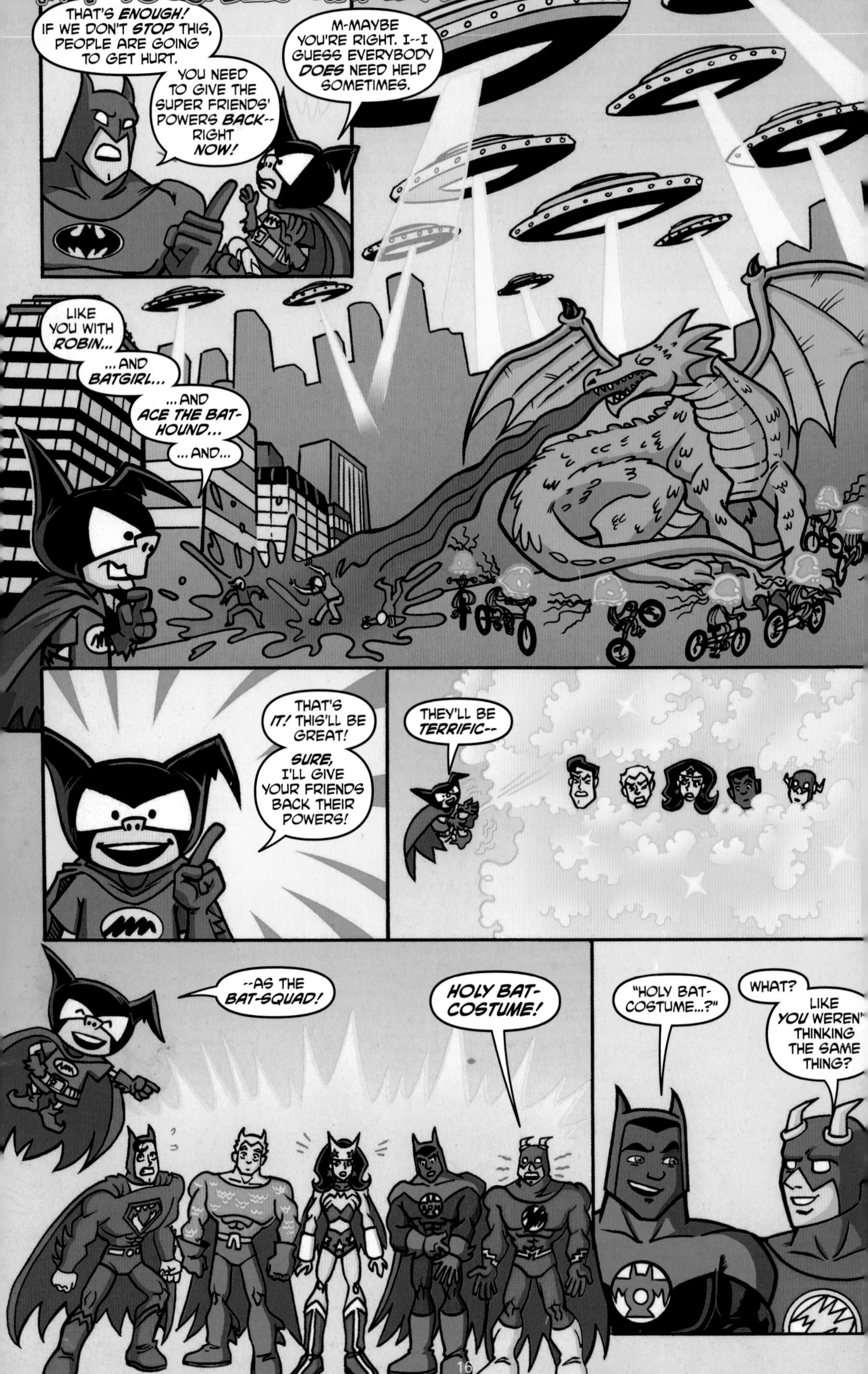

THAT'S ENOUGH! IF WE DON'T STOP THIS, PEOPLE ARE GOING TO GET HURT.
YOU NEED TO GIVE THE SUPER FRIENDS' POWERS BACK-- RIGHT NOW!
M-MAYBE YOU'RE RIGHT. I--I GUESS EVERYBODY DOES NEED HELP SOMETIMES.
LIKE YOU WITH ROBIN...
...AND BATGIRL...
...AND ACE THE BAT-HOUND...
...AND...
THAT'S IT! THIS'LL BE GREAT!
SURE, I'LL GIVE YOUR FRIENDS BACK THEIR POWERS!
THEY'LL BE TERRIFIC--
--AS THE BAT-SQUAD!
HOLY BAT-COSTUME!
"HOLY BAT-COSTUME...?"
WHAT? LIKE YOU WEREN'T THINKING THE SAME THING?

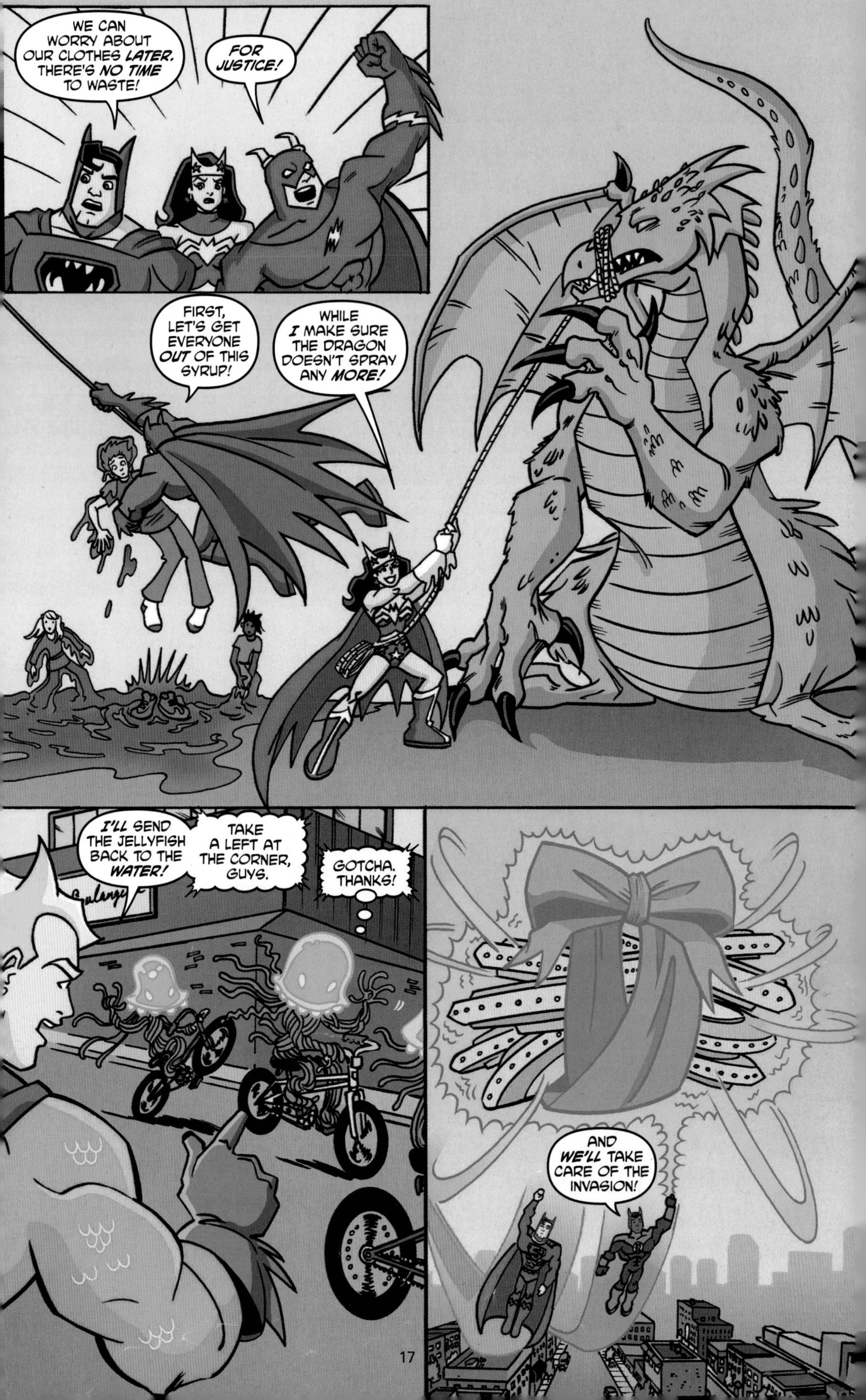
WE CAN WORRY ABOUT OUR CLOTHES LATER. THERE'S NO TIME TO WASTE!
FOR JUSTICE!
FIRST, LET'S GET EVERYONE OUT OF THIS SYRUP!
WHILE I MAKE SURE THE DRAGON DOESN'T SPRAY ANY MORE!
I'LL SEND THE JELLYFISH BACK TO THE WATER!
TAKE A LEFT AT THE CORNER, GUYS.
GOTCHA. THANKS!
AND WE'LL TAKE CARE OF THE INVASION!

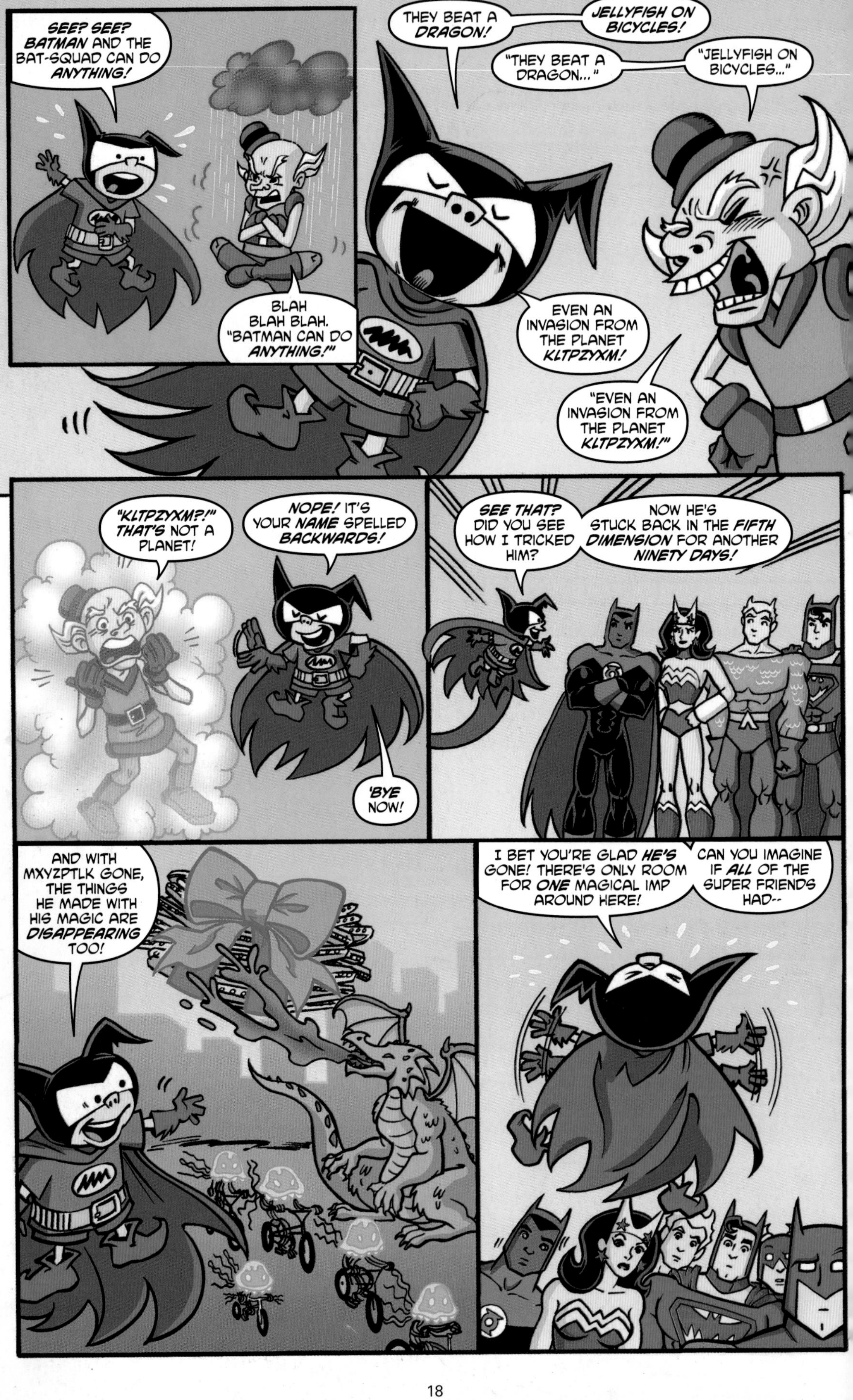
SEE? SEE? BATMAN AND THE BAT-SQUAD CAN DO ANYTHING!
BLAH BLAH BLAH. "BATMAN CAN DO ANYTHING!"
THEY BEAT A DRAGON!
"THEY BEAT A DRAGON..."
JELLYFISH ON BICYCLES!
"JELLYFISH ON BICYCLES..."
EVEN AN INVASION FROM THE PLANET KLTPZYXM!
"EVEN AN INVASION FROM THE PLANET KLTPZYXM!"
"KLTPZYXM?!" THAT'S NOT A PLANET!
NOPE! IT'S YOUR NAME SPELLED BACKWARDS!
'BYE NOW!
SEE THAT? DID YOU SEE HOW I TRICKED HIM?
NOW HE'S STUCK BACK IN THE FIFTH DIMENSION FOR ANOTHER NINETY DAYS!
AND WITH MXYZPTLK GONE, THE THINGS HE MADE WITH HIS MAGIC ARE DISAPPEARING TOO!
I BET YOU'RE GLAD HE'S GONE! THERE'S ONLY ROOM FOR ONE MAGICAL IMP AROUND HERE!
CAN YOU IMAGINE IF ALL OF THE SUPER FRIENDS HAD--

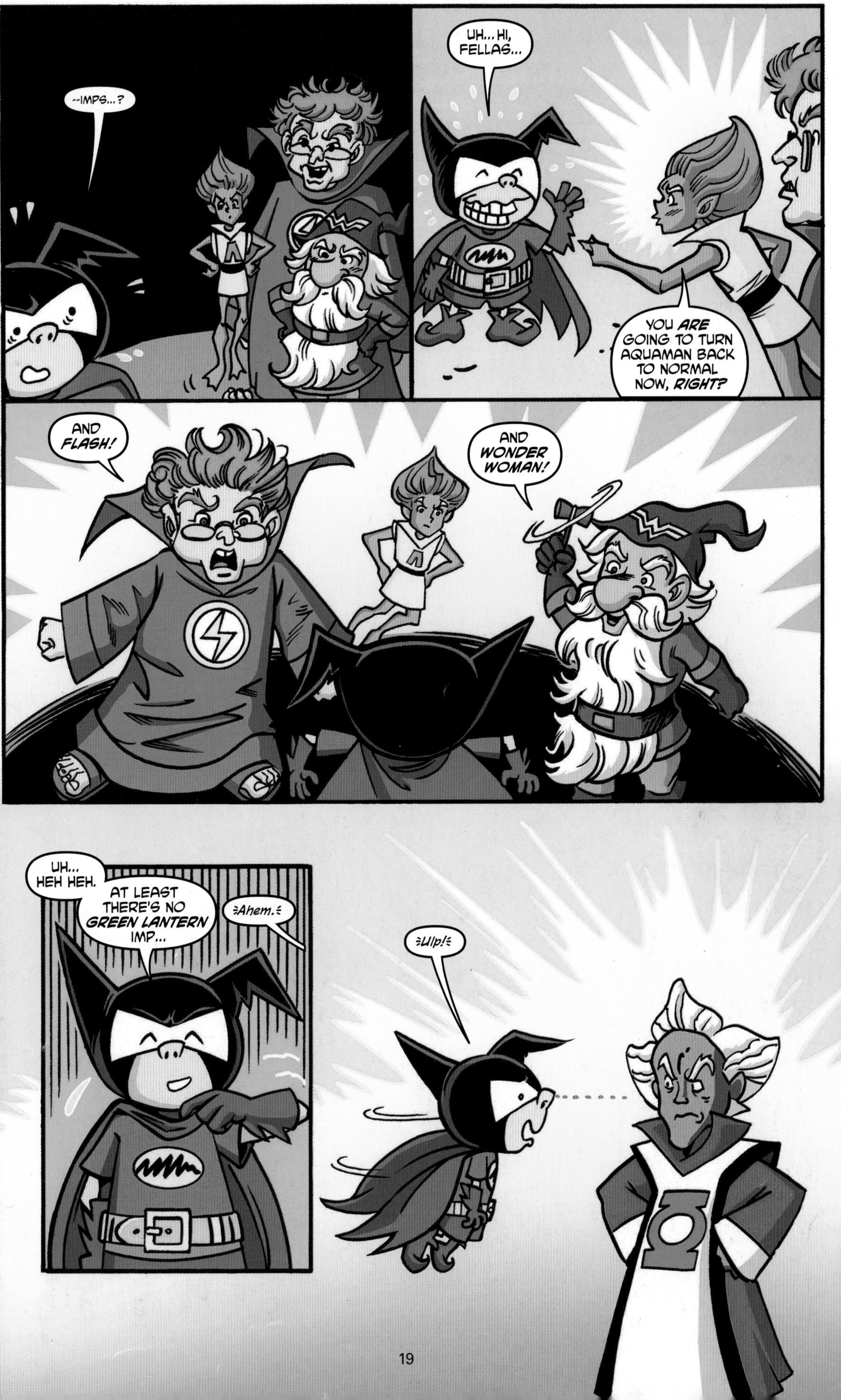
--IMPS...?
UH... HI, FELLAS...
YOU ARE GOING TO TURN AQUAMAN BACK TO NORMAL NOW, RIGHT?
AND FLASH!
AND WONDER WOMAN!
UH... HEH HEH.
AT LEAST THERE'S NO GREEN LANTERN IMP...
Ahem.
Ulp!

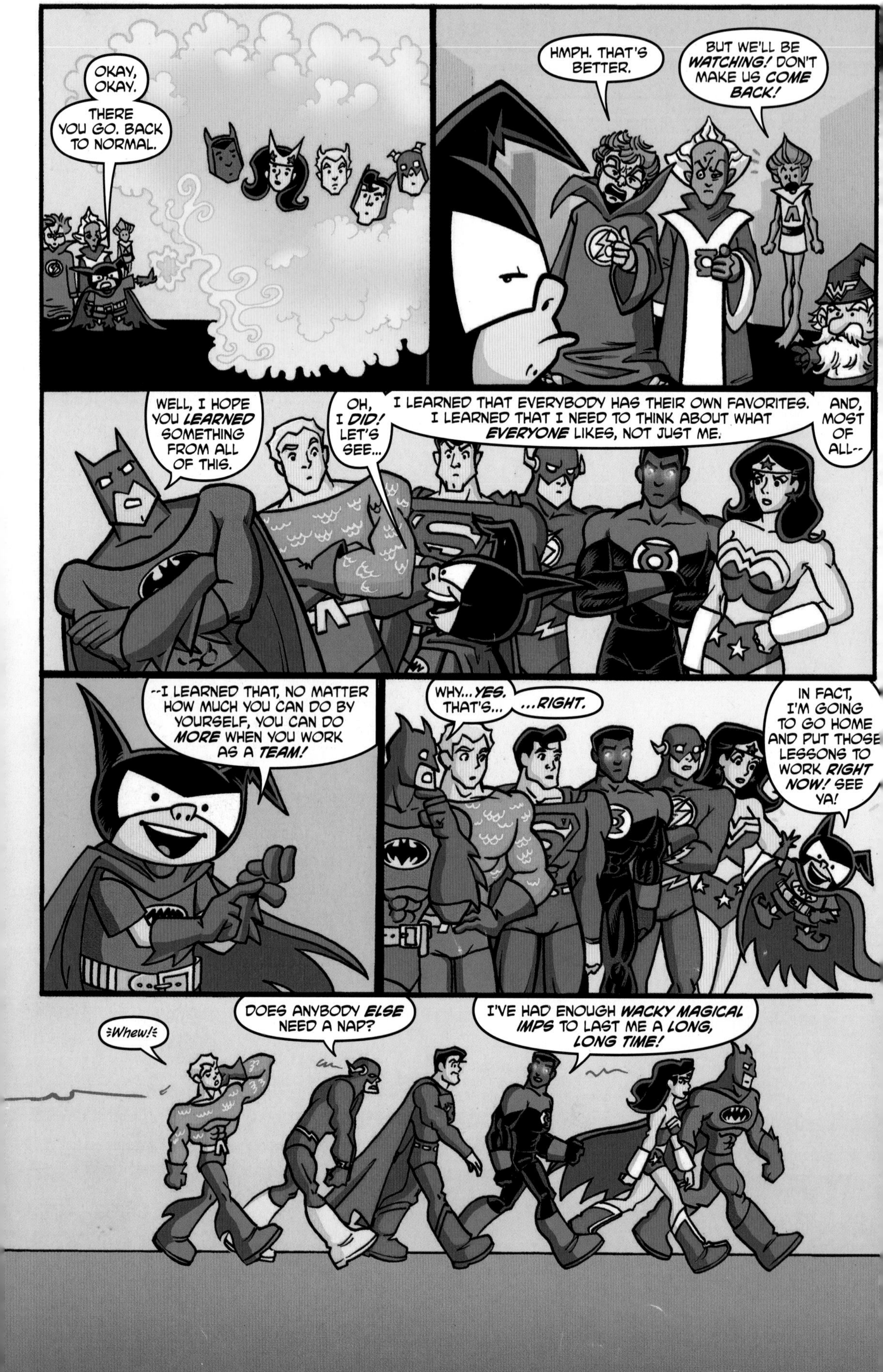
OKAY, OKAY.
THERE YOU GO. BACK TO NORMAL.
HMPH. THAT'S BETTER.
BUT WE'LL BE WATCHING! DON'T MAKE US COME BACK!
WELL, I HOPE YOU LEARNED SOMETHING FROM ALL OF THIS.
OH, I DID! LET'S SEE...
I LEARNED THAT EVERYBODY HAS THEIR OWN FAVORITES. I LEARNED THAT I NEED TO THINK ABOUT WHAT EVERYONE LIKES, NOT JUST ME.
AND, MOST OF ALL--
--I LEARNED THAT, NO MATTER HOW MUCH YOU CAN DO BY YOURSELF, YOU CAN DO MORE WHEN YOU WORK AS A TEAM!
WHY... YES. THAT'S...
...RIGHT.
IN FACT, I'M GOING TO GO HOME AND PUT THOSE LESSONS TO WORK RIGHT NOW! SEE YA!
Whew!
DOES ANYBODY ELSE NEED A NAP?
I'VE HAD ENOUGH WACKY MAGICAL IMPS TO LAST ME A LONG, LONG TIME!

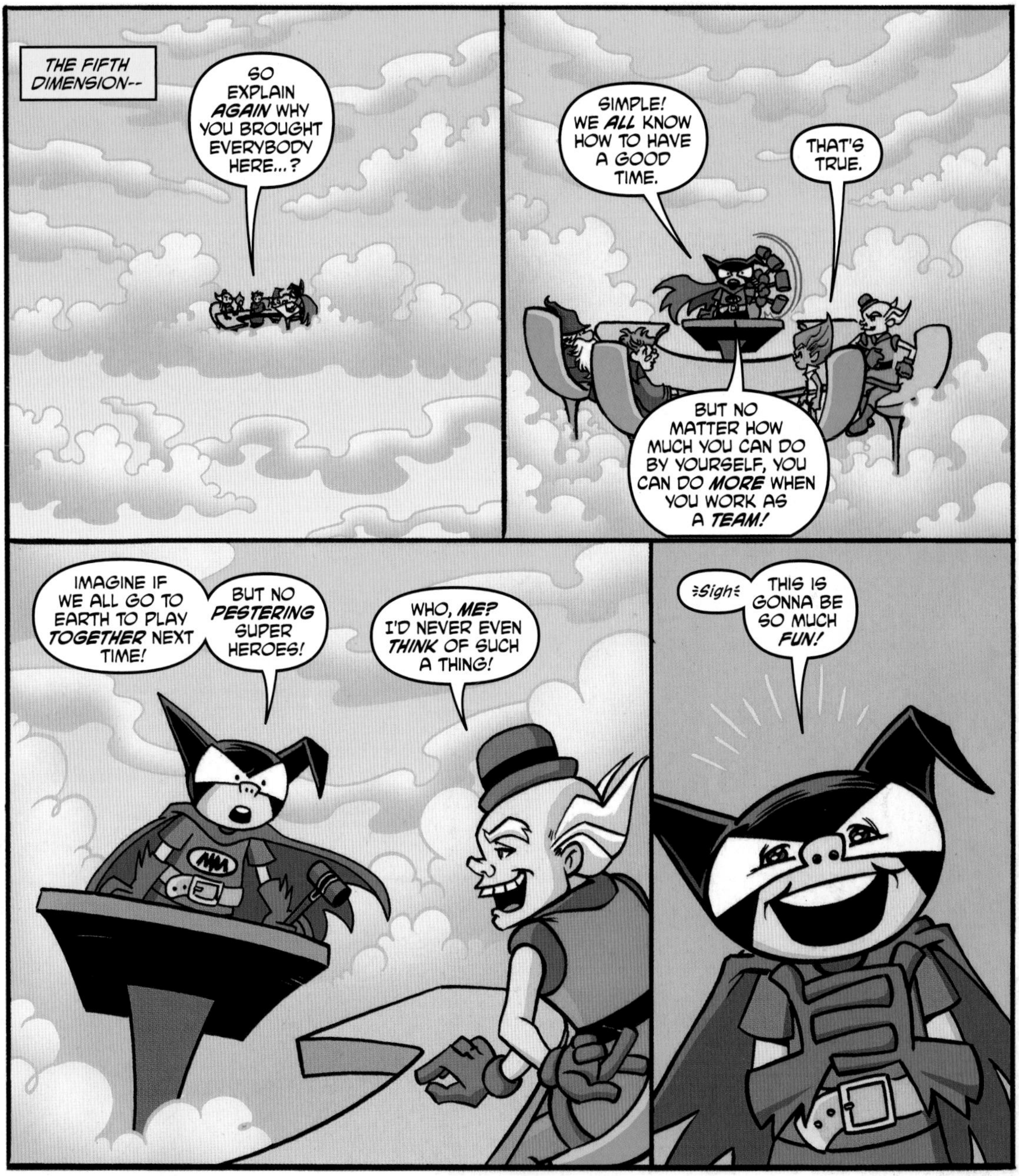
THE FIFTH DIMENSION--
SO EXPLAIN AGAIN WHY YOU BROUGHT EVERYBODY HERE...?
SIMPLE! WE ALL KNOW HOW TO HAVE A GOOD TIME.
THAT'S TRUE.
BUT NO MATTER HOW MUCH YOU CAN DO BY YOURSELF, YOU CAN DO MORE WHEN YOU WORK AS A TEAM!
IMAGINE IF WE ALL GO TO EARTH TO PLAY TOGETHER NEXT TIME!
BUT NO PESTERING SUPER HEROES!
WHO, ME? I'D NEVER EVEN THINK OF SUCH A THING!
Sigh
THIS IS GONNA BE SO MUCH FUN!

NOT THE END!

ATTENTION, ALL SUPER FRIENDS!

HERE'S THIS BOOK'S SECRET MESSAGE:

PEVOY CYSOXRP ZBBU BEI CBY BINOYP

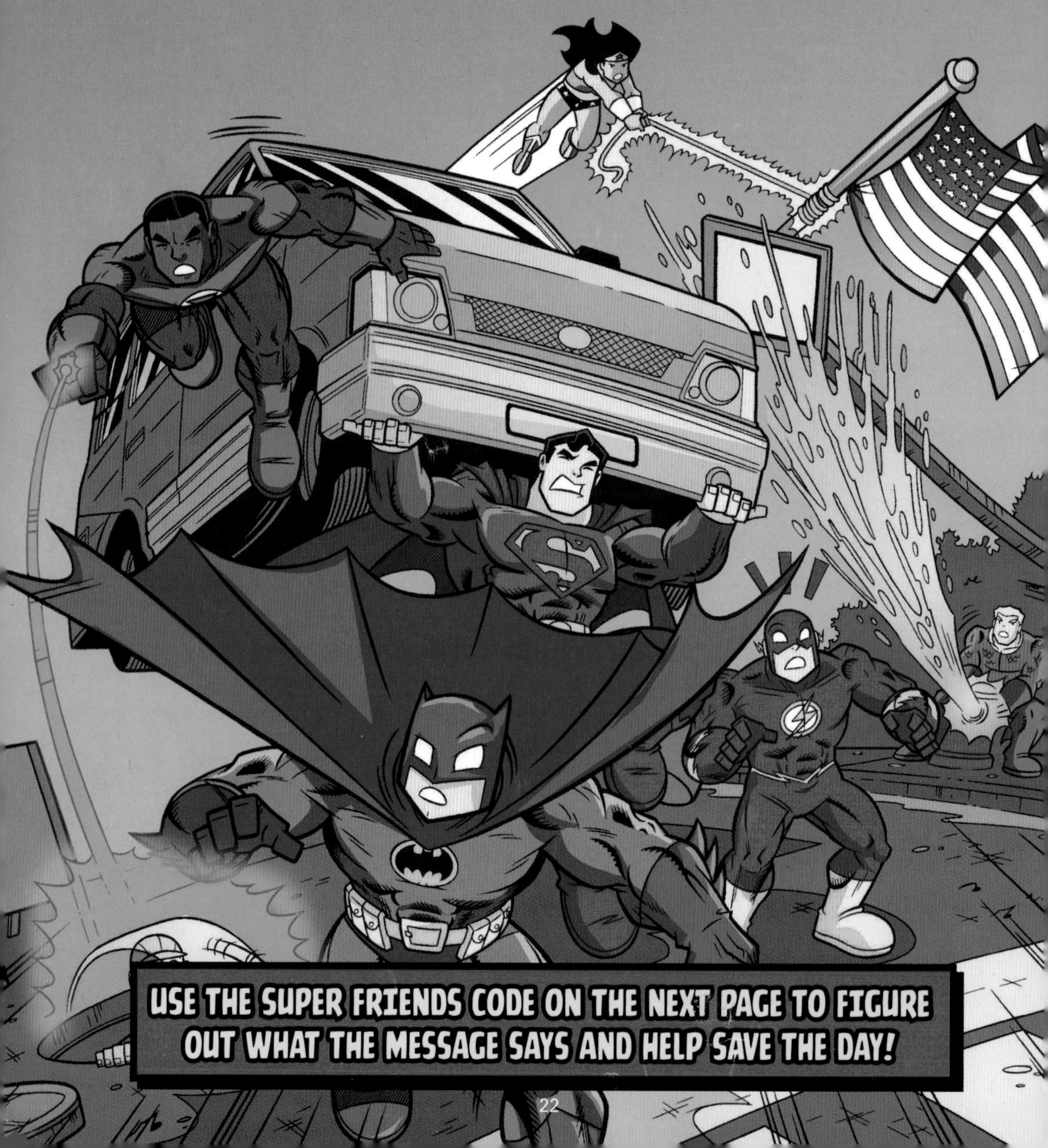

USE THE SUPER FRIENDS CODE ON THE NEXT PAGE TO FIGURE OUT WHAT THE MESSAGE SAYS AND HELP SAVE THE DAY!

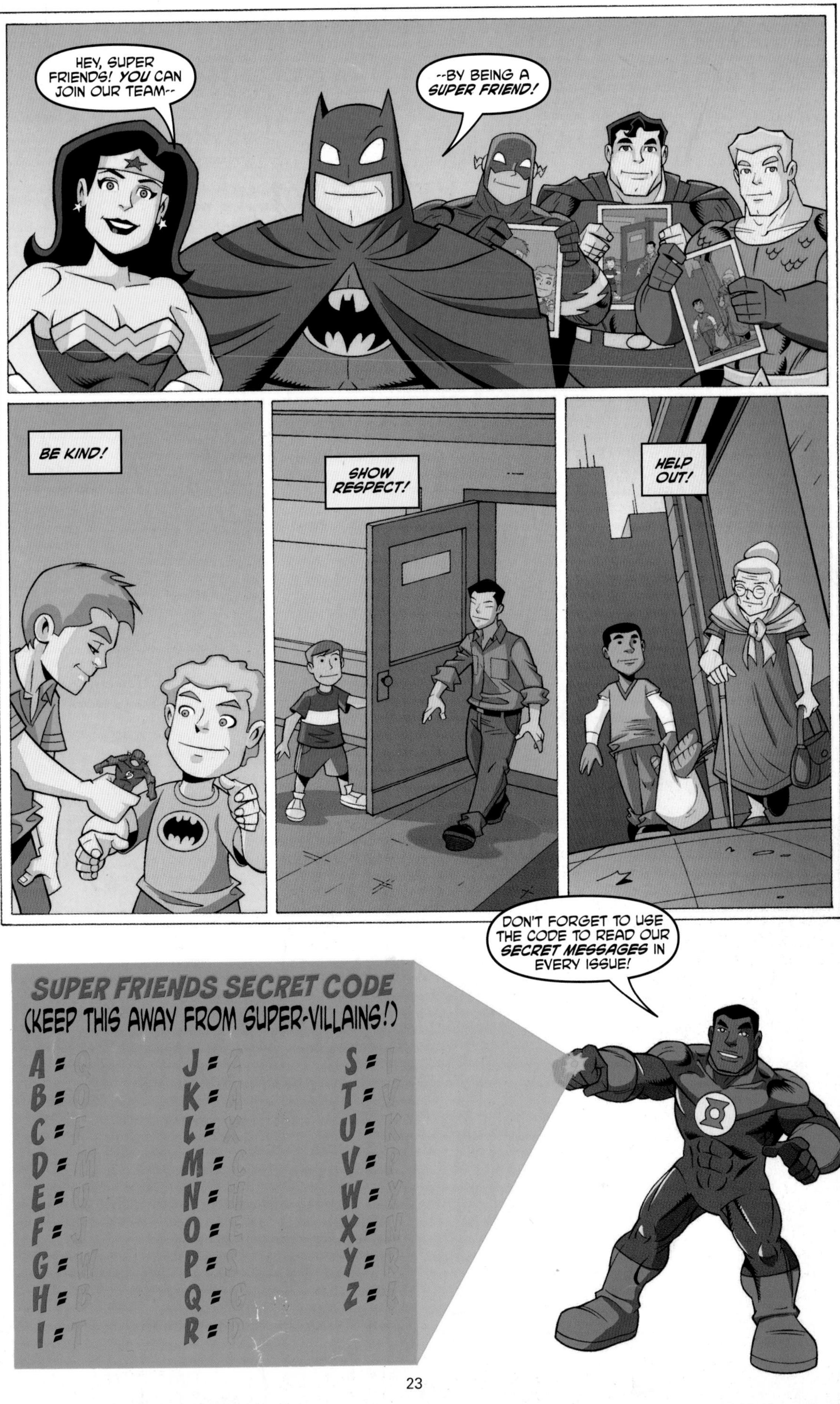
HEY, SUPER FRIENDS! *YOU* CAN JOIN OUR TEAM--
--BY BEING A *SUPER FRIEND!*
BE KIND!
SHOW RESPECT!
HELP OUT!
DON'T FORGET TO USE THE CODE TO READ OUR *SECRET MESSAGES* IN EVERY ISSUE!
SUPER FRIENDS SECRET CODE
(KEEP THIS AWAY FROM SUPER-VILLAINS!)
A = Q
B = O
C = F
D = M
E = U
F = J
G = W
H = B
I = T
J = Z
K = A
L = X
M = C
N = H
O = E
P = S
Q = G
R = D
S = I
T = V
U = K
V = P
W = Y
X = N
Y = R
Z = L

KNOW YOUR SUPER FRIENDS!

SUPERMAN

Real Name: Clark Kent

Powers: Super-strength, super-speed, flight, super-senses, heat vision, invulnerability, super-breath

Origin: Just before the planet Krypton exploded, baby Kal-EL escaped in a rocket to Earth. On Earth, he was adopted by a kind couple named Jonathan and Martha Kent.

BATMAN

Secret Identity: Bruce Wayne

Abilities: World's greatest detective, acrobat, escape artist

Origin: Orphaned at a young age, young millionaire Bruce Wayne promised to keep all people safe from crime. After training for many years, he put on costume that would scare criminals - the costume of Batman.

WONDER WOMAN

Secret Identity: Princess Diana

Powers: Super-strong, faster than normal humans, uses her bracelets as shields and magic lasso to make people tell the truth

Origin: Diana is the Princess of Paradise Island, the hidden home of the Amazons. When Diana was a baby, the Greek gods gave her special powers.

GREEN LANTERN

Secret Identity: John Stewart

Powers: Through the strength of willpower, Green Lantern's power ring can create anything he imagines

Origin: Led by the Guardians of the Universe, the Green Lantern Corps is an outer-space police force that keeps the whole universe safe. The Guardians chose John to protect Earth as our planet's Green Lantern.

THE FLASH

Secret Identity: Wally West

Powers: Flash uses his super-speed in many ways: he can run across water or up the side of a building, spin around to make a tornado, or vibrate his body to walk right through a wall

Origin: As a boy, Wally West became the super-fast Kid Flash when lightning hit a rack of chemicals that spilled on him. Today, he helps others as the Flash.

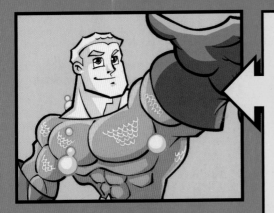

AQUAMAN

Real Name: King Orin or Arthur Curry

Powers: Breathes underwater, communicates with fish, swims at high speed, stronger than normal humans

Origin: Orin's father was a lighthouse keeper and his mother was a mermaid from the undersea land of Atlantis. As Orin grew up, he learned that he could live on land and underwater. He decided to use his powers to keep the seven seas safe as Aquaman.

CREATORS

SHOLLY FISCH WRITER

Bitten by a radioactive typewriter, Sholly Fisch has spent the wee hours writing
books, comics, TV scripts, and online material for more than 25 years. His comic
book credits include more than 200 stories and features about characters
such as Batman, Superman, Bugs Bunny, Daffy Duck, Spider-Man, and Ben 10.
Currently, he writes stories for Action Comics every month, plus stories for
Looney Tunes and Scooby-Doo. By day, Sholly is a mild-mannered developmental
psychologist who helps to create educational TV shows, websites, and other
media for kids.

CHYNNA CLUGSTON ARTIST

Chynna Clugston is a left-handed cartoonist who drinks gallons of tea daily. She
has an obsession with time travel and often wishes everybody would just be
quiet for a few minutes. She's married to her loving husband, Jon Flores.

J. BONE COVER ARTIST

J.Bone is a Toronto based illustrator and comic book artist. Besides DC Super
Friends, he has worked on comic books such as Spider-Man: Tangled Web,
Mr. Gum, Gotham Girls, and Madman Adventures. He is also the co-creator of
the Alison Dare comic book series.

I AM PROGRAMMED TO USE *ALL* OF THE SUPE FRIENDS' ABILITIES. WOND WOMAN'S *STRENGTH*, BATMAN'S *AGILITY*--

GLOSSARY

dimension [di·MEN·shuhn]-a fictional level [or place] of existence, consciousness, or awareness

distractions [di·STRAKT·shuhnz]-things that make it hard to pay attention

genius [JEEN·yuhss]-someone with great natural ability or extraordinary intelligence

imp [IMP]-a small, mischievous person or creature

intellectual [in·tuh·LEKT·choo·uhl]-engaged in or given to learning and thinking

invasion [in·VAY·zhuhn]-entrance of an army into a country for conquest

justice [JUHSS·tiss]-the administration of law

pestering [PESS·ter·ing]-annoying or bothering

ridiculous [ri·DIK·yoo·luhss]-absurd, unrealistic, or silly

scrambled [SKRAM·buhld]-tossed or mixed together

stakes [STAKES]-the consequences or rewards for winning or losing

MY POWER RI
CAN SLOW HI
DOWN!

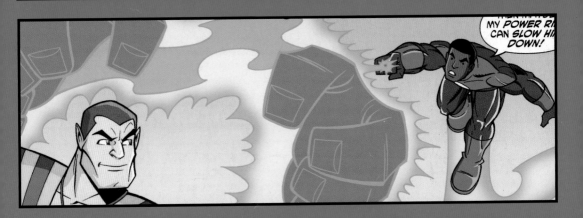

VISUAL QUESTIONS & PROMPTS

1. Whose powers did Batman use to control this octopus?

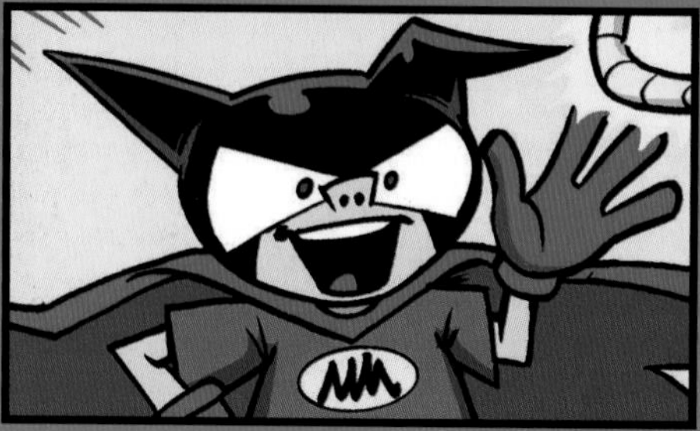

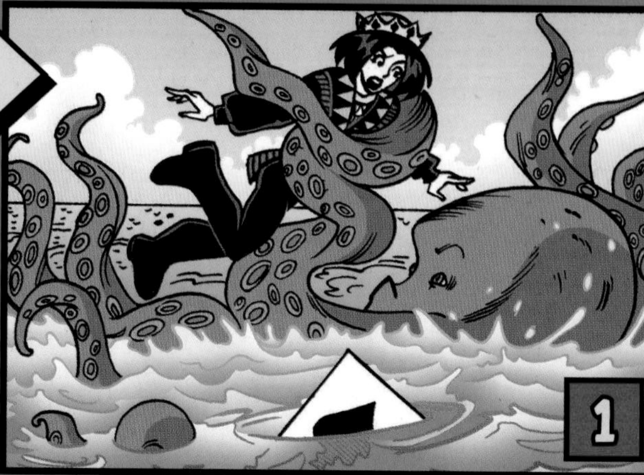
1

2. Why does Bat-Mite overlap the panel borders in this panel? Why do you think the comic book's creators chose to do this? How does it make you feel?

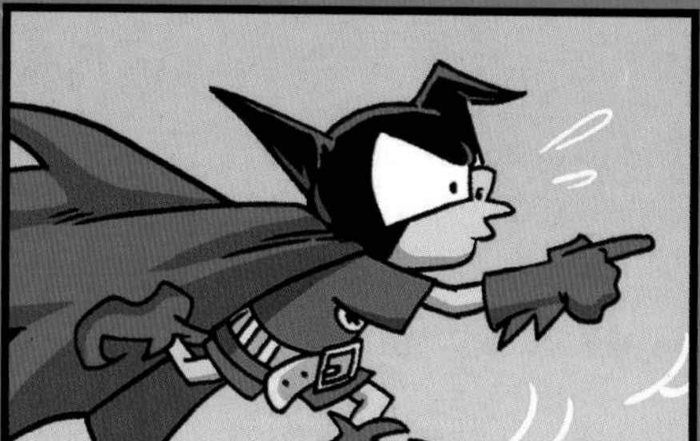

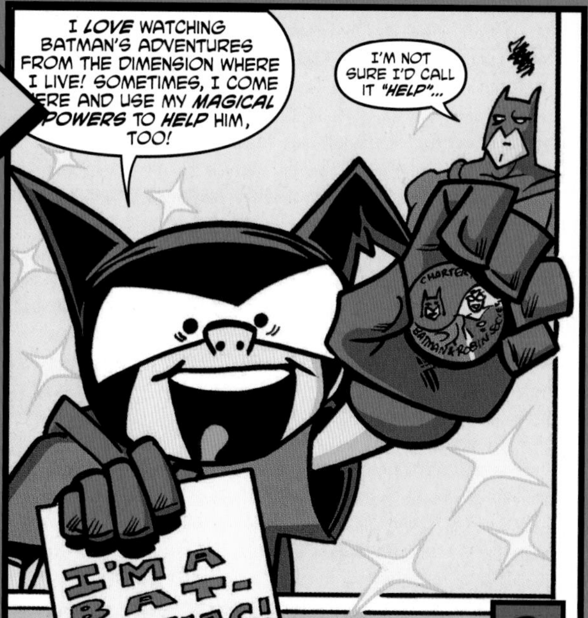
I *LOVE* WATCHING BATMAN'S ADVENTURES FROM THE DIMENSION WHERE I LIVE! SOMETIMES, I COME HERE AND USE MY *MAGICAL POWERS* TO *HELP* HIM, TOO!
I'M NOT SURE I'D CALL IT *"HELP"*...
I'M A BAT-MANIAC!
2

3. What does the dotted red line between these two characters mean?

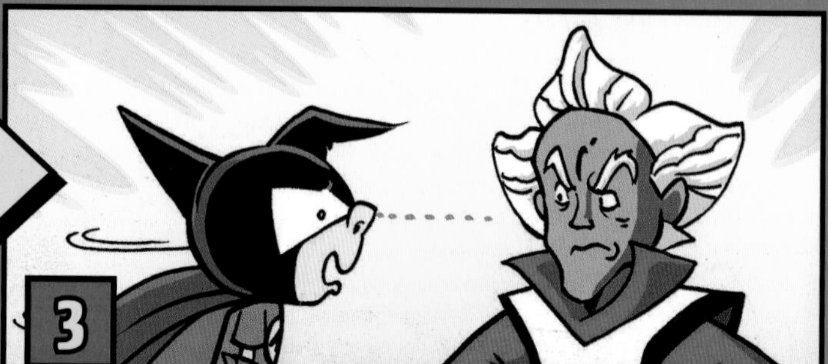
3

4. In this panel, Mr. Mxy creates jellyfish on bicycles. If you had Mxy's powers, what silly combinations would you create?

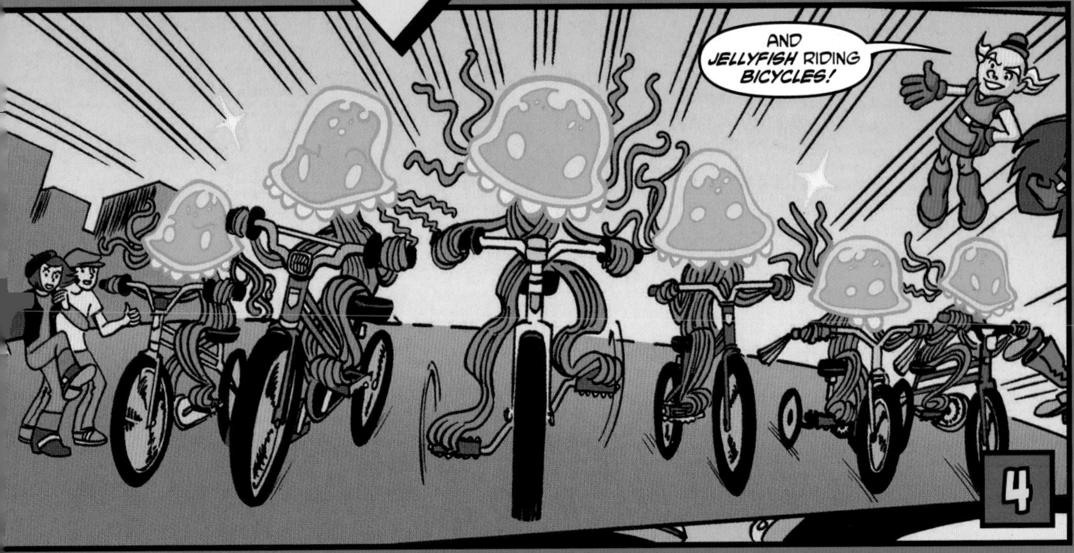
AND *JELLYFISH* RIDING *BICYCLES!*
4

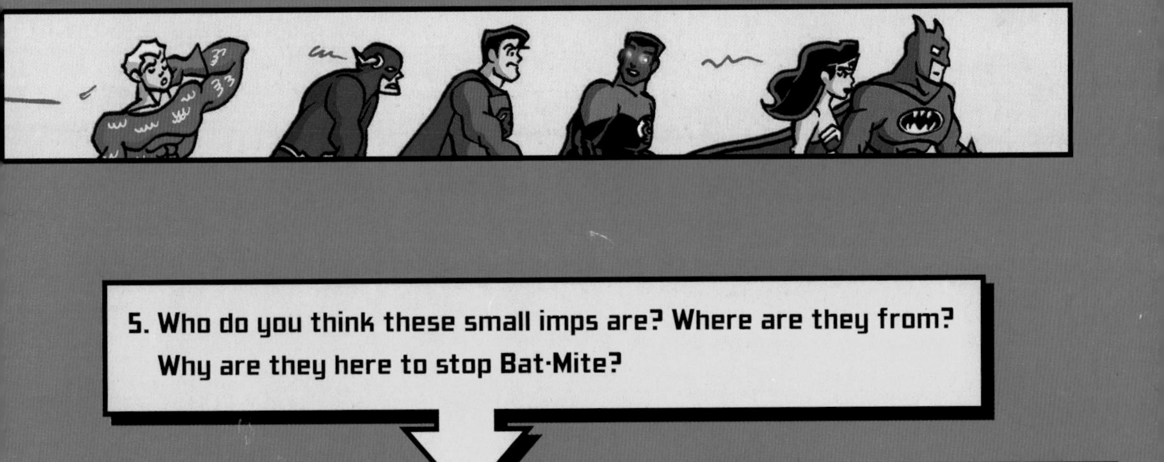

5. Who do you think these small imps are? Where are they from? Why are they here to stop Bat-Mite?

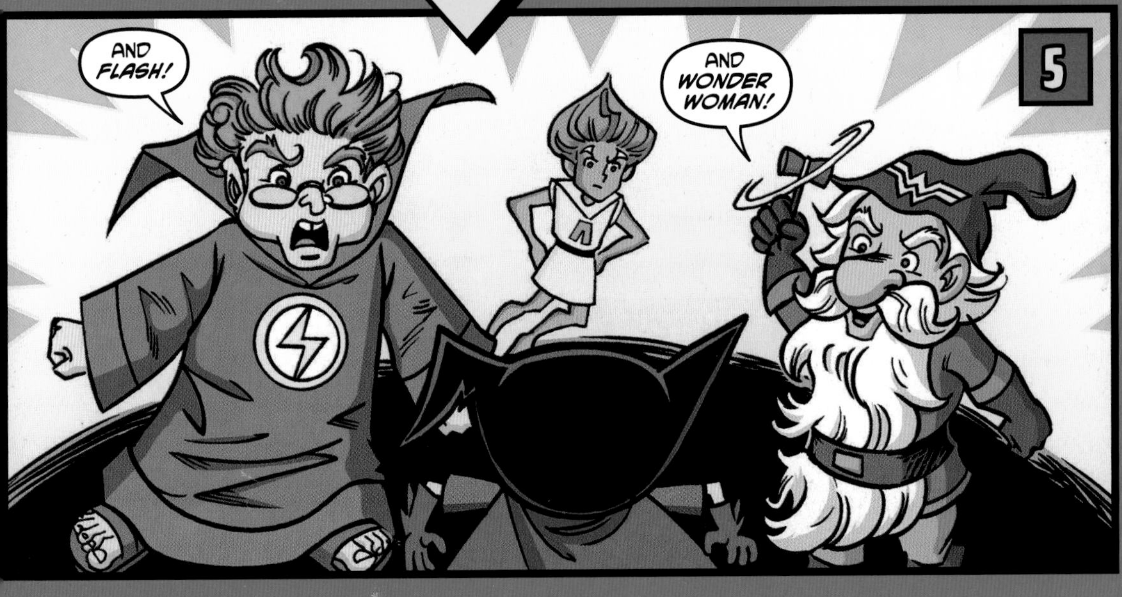
AND *FLASH!*
AND *WONDER WOMAN!*
5

READ THEM ALL!

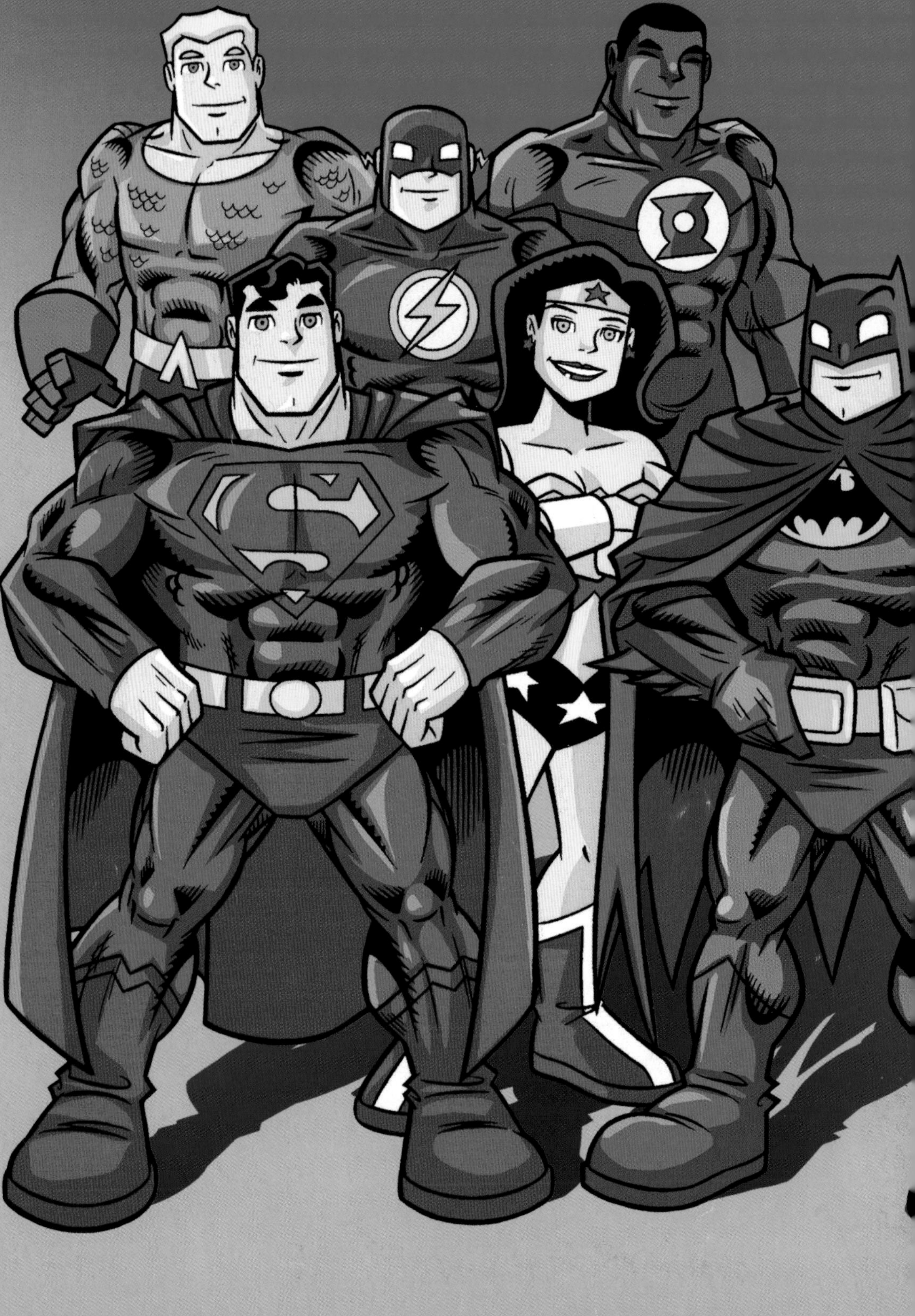

DC SUPER FRIENDS™

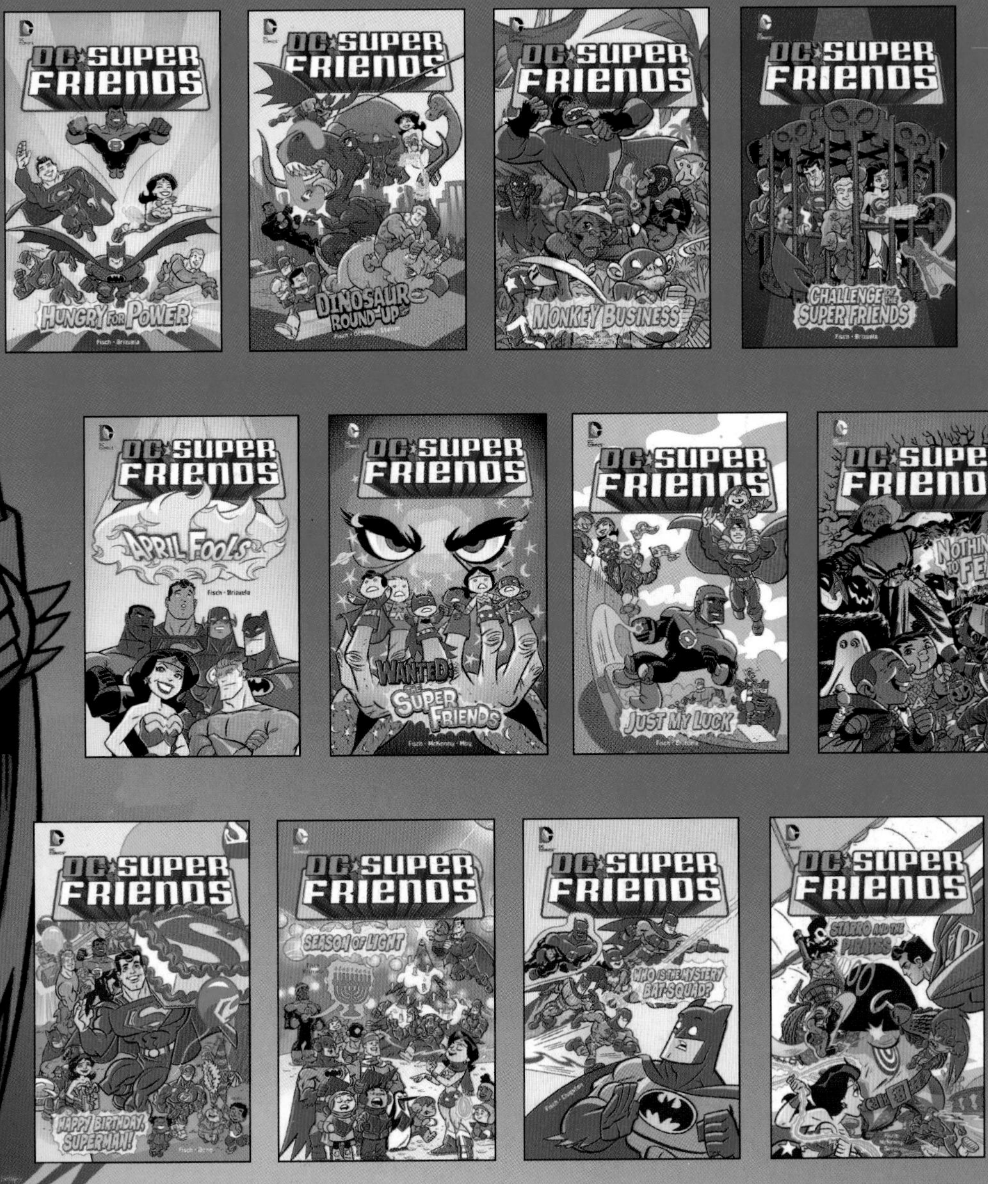
DC SUPER FRIENDS
Hungry for Power
Dinosaur Round-Up
Monkey Business
Challenge of the Super Friends
April Fools
Wanted: Super Friends
Just My Luck
Nothing to Fear
Happy Birthday, Superman!
Season of Light
Who is the Mystery Bat-Squad?
Starro and the Pirates

ONLY FROM...

STONE ARCH BOOKS™

a capstone imprint www.capstonepub.com

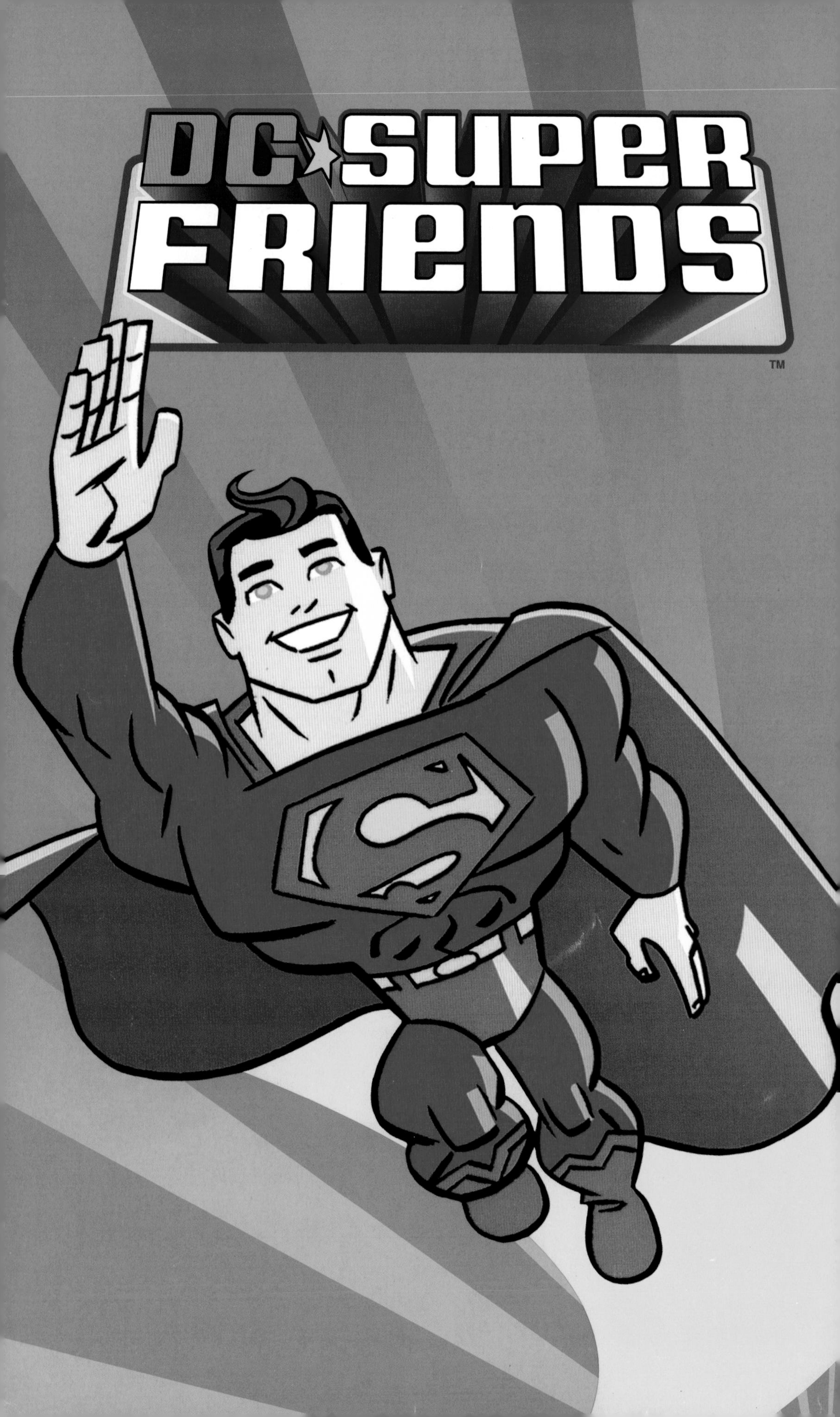
DC SUPER FRIENDS
TM

1/31/17: inside back cover dirty.
WGRL-HQSC